JEWISH STORIES OF PRAGUE

Jewish Prague in History and Legend

By V.V. Tomek

"Jewish Stories of Prague, Jewish Prague in History and Legend" is an English translation and free adaptation of "Prazske zidovske povesti a legendy" by V.V. Tomek, published by Koncel in Prague, Czechoslovakia, in 1932.

ISBN-10: 151178315X

ISBN-13: 978-1511783156

Cover illustration: Mikolas Ales, Rabi Loew and Golem, pen and ink, 1899.

This book does not use Czech diacritical marks.

Published by Sharpless House
Palm Harbor, Florida, United States

CONTENTS

One warm summer evening, I was walking to my home, which is in the centre of Prague. Walking by the Old New Synagogue of Prague, I was suddenly approached by a strange-looking man. Despite the hot weather, he was clad in dark clothes and wore a heavy black hat. I also noticed his beard and side-locks. He was holding an unlit cigarette and spoke in English, "Excuse me, sir, do you have a light?"

"Certainly," I said and handed him my lighter.

"Actually, do you mind lighting the cigarette for me?"

"Sure," I said and did so.

My curiosity won over my shyness, and I asked him, "Do you mind telling me why you couldn't light it yourself?"

He replied, "You see, I'm an Orthodox Jew, and my religion forbids me to handle fire at this time."

The logic of this escaped me. We talked some more, and I learned that he was from Israel but lived in Prague.

After we had bid farewell to each other, I went home, intrigued. I wanted to find out more about Jews and the Jewish faith.

I learned about the 800-year-history of Prague Jews and discovered a beautiful book, The Jewish Prague Legends and Tales, written by V.V. Tomek, published in Czech in 1934.

Now I have the pleasure to offer the book to an English-speaking audience. I have adapted the book to contemporary circumstances, explaining what has become of some of the places mentioned. I have also changed the titles of several chapters. One chapter in particular needed such a change—the chapter originally named "The Greatest Jewish Disaster of the World." It deals with the Prague Easter Pogrom of 1389. When Tomek wrote this book, little did he imagine that yet another, much greater Jewish tragedy was about to happen.

The translator

1. JEWS COME TO PRAGUE

The history of Jews in the Czech lands is still a mystery. Even the greatest historians disagree on when the Jews first arrived in Prague. Jewish written sources were largely destroyed during the numerous Prague fires, especially during the 1560 fire.

For this reason, allow me to give you a few accounts of early Czech Jewish history as described by a handwritten document, which used to be held by the famous Oppenheim Library, but is now the property of the University of Oxford in England.

According to one tradition, a great city had once stood where the city of Prague is today, and many Jews lived there. The ancient city was destroyed, and its citizens dispersed throughout Europe.

The Czech Duchess Libuse founded the city of Prague in 730 A.D. When Libuse was upon her deathbed, she summoned her son Nezamysl and spoke to him thus, "My beloved son, soon I am going to join my ancestors. Before I die, I wish to reveal to you the future. When your grandson rules over this nation of mine, a small and oppressed nation, which believes in only one God, shall seek his protection in this land. Let them be received with hospitality. Let your grandson lend them his

1

protection! For they shall bring a great blessing and prosperity to our land. When more than a hundred years after Libuse's death Duke Hostivit assumed the Czech throne, Libuse appeared in his dream and said, "The time shall soon come for my prophecy to be fulfilled. Before your throne, a small nation, which believes in one God, shall ask for your help. Receive them kindly and render them your protection."

In 850 A.D., the Vends invaded Lithuania and the neighbouring lands and they banished all the country's people into exile. One Jewish community shared this sad fate. The unfortunate exiles wandered through the world without a home.

At last, they arrived in the Czech lands. Tired from their long journey, they asked for an audience with Duke Hostivit. Their request was granted, and they were told to send the two most senior members for the hearing.

The duke received them kindly and asked them, "Who are you and what do you wish of me?"

The two envoys replied, "We are of a small nation that is called Israel, after our forefather. We lived peacefully in one of the Moscow provinces until a powerful enemy forced us to leave. Ever since, we have been wandering through the world without rest. The desert was our bed, stones were our pillows, and the sky was our only roof. We are a peaceful nation, small in numbers and strength. We hold to the teaching of Moses and believe in one God who is omniscient, omnipotent, benevolent, and merciful, and whose grace fills the whole universe.

"Great Duke, let us build our homes here. Your country is large, and your nation is good. We ask you, Great Duke, for your powerful protection. We promise to become your faithful subjects. We shall humbly pray to our God that he lends you and your nation great glory and the stars of victories."

Duke Hostivit knew right-away that they were the nation whose coming was foretold. He said, "Very well. Wait two days for my decision. Come back the day after tomorrow. Then I shall give you an answer."

* * *

The next day, the duke summoned all his elders and chiefs and spoke to them. "Most honourable chiefs and elders! Before her death, my great grandmother Libuse made a prophesy that a small nation seeking our help would enter our land. She appeared in my dreams and told me that the time was near. I was to receive those who are oppressed and who believe in one God, tolerate them in my land, and give them all my protection.

"Yesterday, two men stepped before my throne and asked for my help for their people. They are of the ancient respectable nation of Jews. They ask that they be allowed to live in our land. I have no doubts that these are the people my great grandmother meant. I would like to let them stay and build their homes here, for they shall bring us luck and prosperity. I sent for you, my honourable chiefs and elders, so I can hear your most important voice in the matter. Let me hear your advice."

"Do as you say," was their answer. "Libuse ordered that. Let it be so! This folk shall bring us blessing and luck."

The Czech duke then told the Jewish envoys his decision and instructed them to build their homes on the left bank of the Vltava River, in a place called Ujezd today.

The Jews kept their word. The early Czech chronicler Kosmas tells us that the Prague Jews supported Duke Hostivit with money and supplies, so that he was able to defeat the Germans in his wars with them. Thus, we find Jews were in the Czech lands even during the times of paganism, long before the Faith of Christ became known in the country.

During the reign of Borivoj, who converted to Christianity in 900 A.D., the Prague Jewish community grew so large that their home on the Vltava left bank became very crowded. Therefore, the Jews asked Duke Borivoj to allocate another place for them. The duke let them establish a new Jewish Quarter on the right bank of the Vltava River. The location is called Josefov today. A large area was donated to the Jewish Community of Prague, and even those lacking means were strongly aided by the duke in building their new homes.

Later, the community also received a spacious area near the Jewish Quarter for a Jewish cemetery. The building of the Jewish Quarter of Prague began in 907 A.D.

The Jewish Quarter, or rather the Jewish Town as it was called by the Czechs, at first consisted largely of several dozen wooden houses. As the art of architecture was not available in the Czech lands in those times, building masters and architects were hired from Italy. The only power to be able to undertake such an endeavour was Duke Borivoj and his government—the project was realised under his auspices. The first synagogue of Prague was a simple wooden building. The first Prague rabbi was a man named Malchi. He was born in Cracow and was a great scholar.

The first Jews came to Prague from the region of Moscow and from Poland; they dressed in a Moscow manner and introduced a Polish rite in their synagogue. The Polish rite has been kept in the Old New Synagogue of Prague to this day.

The Jewish Town grew and prospered while it enjoyed the protection of Czech dukes, who conferred many privileges upon the community. More privileges were given to Prague Jews, as they distinguished themselves on various occasions. In 1150, during the reign of King Wladislaus, large processions of flagellants were going through the country, whipping their backs. They challenged the established religion and attempted to convert the nation to their ways, so the king ordered that all flagellants must leave the kingdom at once. The flagellants were too weak to oppose the royal power, so they decided to vent their frustration on the Prague Jews. At night, the Jewish Town was attacked. However, the flagellants met a fierce defence.

Many strongly built Jewish butchers gathered at the first noise. Wielding a huge kosher axe in one hand and a burning torch in the other, they pounced on the raging flagellants.

Although the flagellants outnumbered the defenders, the flagellants were seized by panic and retreated hastily. The Jewish butchers ran after them and chased them out of Prague.

As soon as King Wladislaus heard of this news, he summoned the Jewish butchers for an audience. He thanked them for their courage and praised them for saving the Jewish Town and for chasing the intruders out of the capital city. As a reward, he gave the butchers the privilege to use the two-tailed Czech lion on their coat of arms. This noble privilege was confirmed by all the Czech kings who followed in reigning Bohemia. King Wladislaus also granted the Prague Jews the right to fortify their quarter by walls and gates. The gates were closed at night to prevent such murderous attacks.

After the reign of King Wladislaus up to the reign of King Jiri of Podebrady, Jews lived in relative peace, despite all the unrest that now and again shook the Kingdom of Bohemia.

Now and again, an ugly slander against Jews caused them to be expelled from the kingdom. Every time, they were called back, for it became obvious that such slander stemmed only from envy. Despite their hardships, Jews remained peaceful and dedicated citizens of the Czech lands.

2. THE OLD NEW SYNAGOGUE

The Old New Synagogue of Prague is a truly ancient building. The only older synagogue in Europe is the famous Synagogue of Worms in south-western Germany. There, Jews gathered as early as during the time of the Second Temple. The two synagogues might be the oldest functioning Jewish temples in the world, since the Western Wall of the Jerusalem Temple is considered a ruin by many.

The Old New Synagogue was built in a Gothic-German style, typical of the medieval architecture of Europe. The building consists of three parts—the synagogue for men, one for women, and a small prayer room for those who were too busy to attend the regular services. The two latter parts were most likely added in later times. The synagogue entrance faces the south. Only a few steps lead down to the temple's interior.

For a long time, a small wooden temple had to do for the Jewish community of Prague. As the community grew, the small temple could no longer accommodate the growing numbers.

According to Jewish beliefs, 4690 years after the creation of the universe, i.e. 962 A.D., the community elders decided that a new, spacious synagogue would be built of stone. A small hillock covered by piles of rock and fallen trees was chosen for this purpose.

While digging the new synagogue foundations, the workers hit upon a white stone wall. The wall seemed to be the remnants of an old temple. A further discovery confirmed this—a scroll written on a deerskin parchment and a few prayer books in Hebrew were found on the site.

At that time, two messengers from Jerusalem were in Prague to raise money for the poor in the Holy City. Since these two men were renowned scholars and Talmudists, Rabbi Chisdai of Prague asked them for advice. The Prague Jews hesitated about what to do with the discovered wall. Both messengers said, "Jews must have dwelled here during the times of the Second Temple. It was they who built this structure. Because these stones were once already marked for a sacred purpose, and they are in a good shape, you should use them to build your new synagogue.

"Further, we advise you to build the new synagogue like the one in Tiberias, after the Holy Temple of Jerusalem. You can make the windows Shkufim Atumim, so that they are broad without but narrow within. Also, build a massive arch on two pillars at the synagogue entrance and several steps leading down inside. The synagogue must be built deeper, for it is written, 'From the depths, I call you, O Lord!' If you build the synagogue in such a way, the Almighty shall hear you and shall protect this house of prayer from destruction by fire and water."

Not all members of the Prague Jewish community were happy with this advice. Some thought it a desecration of the memory of the Temple of Jerusalem. However, when the community senior Shlomo Kun was visited by the Prophet Elijah in a dream and told to follow the Jerusalem messengers' instructions, all finally agreed. The messengers then left Prague, carrying rich gifts for the poor of the Holy City.

It is thought that to satisfy those who believed it would be a sacrilege to build in the style of the Temple of Jerusalem; the walls of the new synagogue were painted black as a sign of mourning.

Sirenius, an architect from Saxony, was hired to see the project through. The construction went fast; the building was completed only two years later. In June 931 A.D., during the celebration of Shavuot, a holiday commemorating the day God gave the Ten Commandments to Moses, the synagogue was consecrated and opened.

Some scholars believe that the synagogue was named Old New, because it was built upon the remnants of an old temple. Others explain the synagogue's name by the word of Hebrew origin Altnai, which means "conditional," while sounding as Alt-Neu (Old New) in

German. Another group of historians subscribe to the theory that the Old New Synagogue received its name because the new stone synagogue was built in the place of the old wooden one.

To this day, only a very few changes have been made to the Old New Synagogue's interior. One such change happened in 1784, when a gilded wooden tabernacle was destroyed by a flood. Rabbi Ezekiel Landau ordered that a new tabernacle be made from metal. The Jewish community organized a collection of things made of metal for this purpose. Even the poorest of Jews gave what they could, be it as little as a tin button.

During the thousand years that followed, age covered the synagogue's interior walls with the blackest of dark. Because God's name was written on the walls of the temple, they could never be painted again.

Even the thousand-year-old dust means a sacred past to the Jews, as the synagogue's walls are covered by the noble blood of their fathers.

In 1389 during the reign of Wenceslaus IV, an insane mob attacked the Jewish Town. Old men, women, and children fled to the Old New Synagogue, where they sought refuge. The mob followed them there and broke down the synagogue doors. Then, the attackers demanded that the Jews present either give up their ancient faith on the spot or die. Since none of the faithful Jews did so, they were all murdered—children in front of their mothers, fathers before their sons. The blood of the innocent victims splattered the walls of the Prague temple.

The murderers then fled Prague to Germany. According to old scripts, King Wenceslaus IV sent his officers after the murderous band, but it was too late, and no one was caught. According to other sources, the king let the crime and its perpetrators go without punishment or without even an investigation. The event caused a great commotion among the Czech leaders and among the entire Czech nation.

It is surprising that the Old New Synagogue has survived this and other disasters, including many Prague fires. The synagogue stands to this day. During the horrible fire of 1558, two magnificent white doves were seen upon the top of the synagogue. They waited until the fire was put out and only then flew toward the skies.

The Prague Old New Synagogue has more than sixty curtains, richly decorated by gold and pearls, hanging before the tabernacle. Among them are curtains donated to the Jewish community by Karpel Sachs, the first Parnas (mayor) of the Prague Jewish Town in 1601, and curtains from the famous Yekev Schmiles and his wife.

Yekev Schmiles had the privilege to mint money. He was said to have his own mint in the Jewish Town on the square near the Three Wells. Even today, one can come across his coins, the "Schmiles Thallers." His tomb and the tomb of his wife can be found in the Old Jewish Cemetery in Prague.

Kosmas, an early Czech chronicler, tells about crusaders that went through the Czech lands forcing baptisms and murdering Prague Jews. Kosmas writes that the Prague Archbishop wanted to prevent the tragedy but was unable to do so because the Duke of Prague and his guards were not present in the capital. Dalimil, another Czech chronicler, writes that the Jews of Prague were able to defend themselves against the crusaders with the king's help.

According to historian Steinherz, the murdering of Jews took place in May 30-31, 1096. This scholar gives a report of persecution of Jews in Germany and Bohemia during the First Crusade. Perhaps the most important account was written by Solomon bar Simeon, who lived in Mainz, Germany at the time of the First Crusade. He most likely refers to Prague when he says that in the city, he calls Shell or Veshell in Hebrew, the Jews, threatened by the crusaders, asked the ruler for help. The ruler sent more than a thousand of his men, and with this assistance the Jews were able to stand up against the crusaders and afterwards move to the right bank of the river into safety.

Another city where Jews fought the crusaders was

Mainz in Germany.

4. JACOB, THE BISHOP'S LIEUTENANT

Jacob was a Jew who converted to Christianity and was baptised. Because of this and favour by Wladislaus, the Czech ruler, he climbed in the church's hierarchy. He became a vicedominus, the Bishop's Lieutenant, which was the second highest ecclesiastical office in Bohemia then. Yet, not even this high office could save him from a fatal fall in the end.

As his power and wealth grew, so did the number of those who coveted his office. They used the fact that he was born a Jew as a tool of their attack. First, a campaign against him was begun by circulating aspersions that Jacob rose with the help of Satan. Even Kosmas, a Czech chronicler, wrote in his chronicle that Jacob was frequently visited by Satan in human form.

Then, Jacob was accused of destroying a Christian altar in a former synagogue and of casting the altar into a cesspit. He was arrested and charged with sacrilege. Sacrilege was a capital crime then, and anyone who would dare commit it would surely have to be insane, so it was very unlikely that the vicedominus had done such a deed. Yet, he was tried and sentenced to death. He was stripped of his office, and his entire property was confiscated. He escaped the executioner only after the

Prague Jewish community raised three thousand pounds of silver and one hundred pounds of gold as money for his ransom.

Jacob was expelled from Bohemia, and the ruler was said to use the money to free Christian slaves who served Jews as poor Goyim (gentiles). In addition, the ruler issued a decree that no gentile was to serve Jews thereafter. This happened in 1120.

In those times, such cases were not rare. A crime was committed, and Jews were blamed for it. This was especially so in politics, which was a nasty business, and where the lowest tricks were often the most efficient ones. Despite such occurrences, the Prague Jews played a very important role in centralizing the government of Bohemia.

5. THE CONVENT OF ST. MARY MAGDALENE

In the Prague Lesser Town in the street of Karmelitska stands the former Nosticz Palace, which has been recently renovated and today hosts the Mandarin Oriental Hotel of Prague. In its place was once the Church of St. Mary Magdalene. As early as 1329, a convent of St. Mary Magdalene was founded near the church. The Magdalenite nuns were called White Sisters because of the white habits they wore. The Church and Convent of St. Mary Magdalene burned to the ground during the Hussite wars in 1420, and the White Sisters never returned.

The church was eventually rebuilt and donated to the Dominican Order in 1604. With the help of numerous sponsors, the Dominicans bought several adjacent houses. A new church and monastery were constructed. They were some of the most magnificent buildings in Prague. The new church was built by the baroque architects Francesco Carrati, Jan de Capuli, and Krystof Dienzenhofer.

The church and monastery served their purpose only for the next hundred years. During the reign of Emperor Joseph II, many monasteries were expropriated and closed by the Imperial Government. The church and monastery of St. Mary Magdalene were closed in the summer of 1783 and sold in 1787. The beautiful church was bought by the Crown of Austria for a mere twenty-four thousand ducats in 1791 and served as a post office until 1849. Six years later, the church became gendarmerie barracks, and later also housed the government printing works.

Many legends and ghost sightings relate to this place. The old church is associated with the Jews because one legend claims that Vicedominus Jacob, mentioned in the previous chapter, dwelled in the church and secretly converted it to a synagogue, for which he was to pay for with his life.

Another legend says that now and again, a procession of white-clad figures can be seen coming out of the Nosticz Palace at night. A few Lesser Town night passers-by said that they had seen apparitions clad in white habits, from which only death-head eyes stared.

6. THE GOLDEN LANE BRIDE

Not much remains of the labyrinth of small lanes and corners of the Old Jewish Town of Prague today. Most of the Jewish Town was put to sword, or rather to demolition crews by the Sanitation Act of 1893. Those who had enacted the law did so with good intentions— the condition of a large part of Josefov, the Old Jewish Town of Prague, was such that a major renovation was badly needed. Many decrepit and small houses were never built to last this long and lacked basic plumbing and other amenities. In addition, Josefov was then at the Vltava River level, and was often flooded.

The Prague City Council intended to remodel this part of the Czech capital after the style of Paris. Where once stood an old ghetto, there are now broad boulevards flanked by majestic Art-Noveau buildings. However, this happened much to the chagrin of the Old Prague enthusiasts, who to this day complain that much of the Old Jewish Town charm was lost to the insensitive hand of an urban renewal project.

The Old Jewish Town of Prague was unique, and the magic of its bizarre streets and lanes can only be found in old paintings and photographs. One of the most noteworthy places of Josefov was a lane called Uzka, originally known as the Golden Lane. It is not clear why it used to be called that. However, the following strange tale might explain such a name: In Rejdiste, an area by the Vltava River bank, facing the Letna Plain on the other bank, once lived a rich and kind Jew by the name of Kalman. He was a widower, and the only consolation of his old age was his beautiful daughter Hanina. He watched after her like a hawk. His chest heaved with pride when many young men rested an admiring eye on her in the Old New Synagogue. Yet, none gathered enough courage even to approach Hanina. Her heavenly beauty and noble demeanour kept would be suitors away.

No one suspected that her heart was already taken. She was in love with a young man whom no one else knew. Not even the old Kalman had a clue why his daughter Hanina always rushed to the Vltava riverbank in the evenings. Her young lover always arrived on a boat, it seemed, from across the river. When the lovers' meeting was over, the river calmed as if to let Hanina's secret lover cross it smoothly. She never saw him reach the opposite bank, as she rushed home.

A betrayal lurked nearby. One of Hanina's admirers from the Old New Synagogue followed her and witnessed her rendezvous with the mysterious stranger. The jealous suitor decided to put an end to the love affair and went to see the old Kalman right-away. The old Kalman ran like a maniac around his living room when the suitor told him that he had seen his daughter Hanina embracing a man clad in a green tailcoat and wearing a pointed hat.

The same evening, Kalman and the suitor, Izim was his name, secretly followed Hanina to the riverbank so that they could catch her and her seducer in the act. The father and the suitor soon both reaped their reward—one that they would not have dreamt in their worst nightmares.

Hanina's sharp-eyed lover saw her followers and begged her to run away with him. In the last moment, when Hanina almost consented, her father stepped in. Grabbing Hanina by her hand, he dragged her home, away from her lover. At his house, they were already expected by an assembly of guests, among them Izim's parents, who were there to celebrate their son's engagement to the beautiful Hanina.

Hanina could not stop crying. She hid in her room and from her window saw her poor lover row his boat away from the riverbank only to jump in the river in the middle of it. As if she lost her mind, she ran out of the house. Overcoming the force of those who tried to stop her, she ran to the river and called her lover. When her father ran after her to bring her back home, she cast herself into the cold waves of the Vltava River.

After Kalman and his guests had witnessed this, they called local boatmen and swimmers to search for Hanina and to rescue her or to find her dead body. Nevertheless, the river waves that stole Hanina never gave her back. Despite all the effort, her dead body was never found.

Her desperate father now deeply regretted his rashness and cursed all the whisperers who had advised him to force his daughter to marry Izim. Kalman became even more generous in his charity. He gave what he could to the poor of Prague, saying like his ancestor Abraham, "What good are worldly goods if I have no children..."

Nevertheless, even his well-known generosity helped him little now. Two years passed, and Kalman grew weak in his grief; illness mercilessly threatened his very being.

* * *

One afternoon, Mrs. Siffres, Kalman's sister and a midwife by profession, was looking out of her window in Narrow Street. The afternoon sun tickled her face, and she almost fell asleep. Suddenly, she noticed a small black cat on the opposite house roof. The cat was pregnant and ran back and forth on the roof, mewing mournfully.

The midwife tried to call the cat, but the cat responded by mewing even more sadly.

"Poor thing," she thought. "If only I knew whose cat she is, then I could help her." Because it was late, she left the window and went to her kitchen to make dinner.

After it grew dark, Mrs. Siffres looked out of the window. The cat was gone. A quiet night came and everyone and everything slept. At midnight, her doorbell suddenly rang. Mrs. Siffres quickly got up, and speaking from the window, she asked the visitor whether he needed her assistance.

"Please come right-away and help my wife. She's in labour," a man's voice sounded from the street. After getting ready, the midwife went to meet him at the door.

"To whom are we going?" she asked.

"Just follow me and we will be there soon," was his answer.

Mrs. Siffres followed the stranger silently. Soon they were at the riverbank. Here, her unknown visitor asked her to step into his boat. She hesitated, so he led her in the boat almost by force. The boat shoved off the bank.

The poor midwife almost fainted from fear. Just when the boat was in the middle of the river, it violently turned as if in a whirlpool and dropped down only to come to rest on the river bottom. The midwife saw a small but magnificent palace. Was she just dreaming?

"This is my home," the stranger said. "Enter without fear, and I will reward you royally."

She entered the palace, and she was almost blinded by the gold, silver, and precious stones sparkling everywhere around her.

"Here is my wife. She needs your help," said the man and opened a door leading to a bedroom. The midwife stepped in, and she could not believe her eyes. In the bed lay the beautiful Hanina.

"My dear Lord!" the midwife exclaimed. "Is it really you, Hanina? You didn't drown in the Vltava?"

It was Kalman's Hanina. She explained to the midwife what had happened. "As soon as I fell in the water, someone caught me in his gentle arms. I saw it was my lover. He thanked me with love and gratitude. He thanked me for withstanding a difficult trial of love and for freeing him from long-suffering and pain. He said, 'Know that I am the Water Sprite of the Vltava River. I had fallen into disgrace with the powerful sprite of the entire world. He had condemned me to exile, which would last a thousand years unless I found a girl who would follow me to my water kingdom. Only then could I get back my inheritance—the Vltava and Labe rivers. Of many, you were the only girl who would rather perish in the waves than give up her love for me.'"

The decisive moment for Hanina arrived. She gave birth to an adorable baby boy. As soon as the child cried for the first time, his father, the water sprite, entered the bedroom, followed by naiads, water nymphs. How much they admired the baby water sprite, held him, and wished him the best of luck in his life!

Soon the father and his naiads left, and Mrs. Siffres

was left alone with Hanina. Hanina shared her fate with her, "In the beginning, I loved being here. My husband loved me tenderly, and the water nymphs were always helpful and fulfilled all my wishes. However, I began to get bored. I missed human company. Finally, my husband allowed me to visit the land world in the form of a black cat. And now you are with me, and I feel much better already."

"I'm very happy that you are alive and well," said Mrs. Siffres. "I 'm glad that I was able to help you in a moment of pain. But let me go back home now."

"Certainly, I cannot keep you here against your wishes," said Hanina and added, "Let me give an advice, though. When my husband offers you a reward, take nothing except for a pile of coal."

The water sprite then entered the bedroom again and asked the midwife to choose her reward. Mrs. Siffres followed him through several rooms full of jewels of gold, precious stones, and pearls. Keeping Hanina's words in mind, she only collected a pile of coal in the last room. Then, she was on her way home. Again, she stepped in the boat, which rose and in no time pushed to the riverbank.

"You can never tell anyone of this," the Vltava Water Sprite warned. "Otherwise, you will meet with a bad end!"

Mrs. Siffres promised him her silence. She jumped

on the riverbank and hurried home to Narrow Street. In her rush, she tripped over something and spilled some of the coal on the ground. She did not bother to pick it up and instead walked home even faster.

At home, her husband, Mr. Siffres, who was used to her being often gone because of her job, still gave her a strange welcome, "Where have you been? I was really worried about you. You know you have been gone for two whole days!"

"Two days?" she mumbled incredulously. Then she remembered her promise to the sprite. She excused herself somehow and went to sleep.

* * *

Next morning, the Siffreses were woken up by an unusual din from the street below. Crowds of people rushed to the Vltava riverbank. Some came back, complaining.

Mrs. Siffres went to the kitchen to prepare breakfast. There she discovered a pile of gold by the fireplace, where she had put the coal the night before.

While Mr. Siffres was awed by this, his wife now understood the reason so many ran to the riverbank. Someone must have found a few pieces of solid gold where she had spilled the coal. People dug in the place but found no more.

"Just keep quiet about this," she told her husband. "No one must find out where the gold comes from. Even you must not know. Let's keep what we have and be glad about it."

The husband wisely listened to his wife's words. They lived well and bought the house in which they were living as tenants. They even had some gold left, hidden by the fireplace.

* * *

Once Mrs. Siffres walked in the Golden Lane—people now called the street that after the gold had been found there. Lo and behold, she saw the old Kalman. Hanina's father looked as if he would not have much longer to live. His face bore witness to his suffering; it was yellow and deeply wrinkled.

She felt great pity for the old man. Trying to cheer him up, she told him that his daughter was well and living elsewhere.

"Where?" he breathed, as if his life depended on her answer.

"I really can't tell you, but it's true," she replied.

The poor old man began to beseech her desperately to tell him more. Because five years had passed since she had seen Hanina, Mrs. Siffres thought that her promise to the water sprite might have expired with the time.

At last, she relented and told Hanina's father that his

28

daughter was the wife of a powerful water sprite. "She is alive. I can't tell you anything more."

When Mrs. Siffres returned home, instead of gold she found a pile of coal in the kitchen. She and her husband were lucky enough to have their house already.

The old Kalman lost his mind from grief. Until his death, he walked on the Vltava riverbank for hours, calling his daughter, all in vain.

7. ONLY FOUR WORDS

This happened in 1394 during the time of King Wenceslaus IV. Historians gave this king the nickname of "Lazy." Many bad things have been written about this unhappy ruler, some true, others perhaps not so. Schiller, the German poet, said about Wenceslaus IV, "Hounded by both, respect and hate, his character staggered throughout history."

Indeed, historical sources give contradictory accounts about the king. On the one hand, he is described as a man of great energy and intellect. On the other hand, he is described as a violent brute, who throughout his life let himself be ruled by his lechery and other unbridled passions. Whatever the truth is, one thing has been documented enough: King Wenceslaus spent more time at drinking and hunting parties than at his sovereign's desk.

It is therefore hardly surprising that law and order were not in good shape during his reign. That many of the high nobles only profited from their offices and instead of public good thought only of their pockets was a result of Wenceslaus's poor governing. Among the victims of a corrupt system, which these men put in place, were Jews. As often before and after, Jews were targeted for extortion.

The Jews of Prague had prospered greatly during the reign of Charles IV, the father of Wenceslaus IV. In contrast to his son, Charles was an exceptionally competent ruler. He saw to it that law and order were always kept. Under his reign, the country thrived as never before, and the commerce of Prague grew, while it enjoyed the powerful protection of the Czech Crown.

The happy times ended when Wenceslaus IV assumed the Czech throne. In the beginning, the king paid little attention to the Prague Jews. Soon, his greedy officials, who no longer felt the strict authority of the Crown above them, saw Jews as a good source of easy enrichment. By imposing arbitrary taxes on the Jewish community and constant attacks on Jewish wealth, they soon deprived the Jews of Prague of the fruits of their previous hard work and thrift. Slowly but inadvertently, Jews became poor. The Jews were not the only ones suffering financially because of King Wenceslaus IV.

The once blossoming commerce was dying. This was due in part to the king's open hostility toward German speakers and other foreigners in the kingdom. This proved disastrous. The royal coffers were soon empty. Suddenly, the king, who himself was always in financial troubles, had an idea how to refill his coffers.

In 1390, the king issued a decree declaring all Christian debts with Jews invalid. He further ordered that a twenty percent tax of such debts be paid to the Crown instead. This meant that Jews lost all the money they had lent to Christian debtors. Many of such debts there were! In those times, Christians, especially those in Prague, loved living on credit. Overnight, the new law rendered the Jews of Prague beggars.

Nevertheless, not even such an unjust law brought much broche (blessing), to the Crown. In 1394, the Royal Treasury was desperately empty again. Because, as a French saying goes, "Appetite grows with food," Jews were to be the ones to fill the treasury again.

* * *

One July day in the unhappy summer of 1394, the Parnas (mayor of the Prague Jewish Town) was summoned to the Old Town Hall. There he was informed by a king's lieutenant that, within eight days, the Prague Jewish community was to pay twenty thousand golden ducats to the Royal Treasury. The king's aide said, "If you fail to do so, not only will there be the harshest of punishments, but the Crown won't be able to guarantee the safety of your community. You know what that means. We all certainly want to prevent such a situation, don't we?"

That day laments filled the Jewish ghetto after the news spread. It was clear what the veiled threat meant—

Jewish blood would be spilled, their property would be ruined, and their houses set on fire. The Jewish mayor called a joint meeting of elders of the community and Prague synagogues. For five days and sleepless nights, no answer was found. The heads of all families were also called; perhaps someone would have an idea of what to do.

The meeting produced no results, so the mayor ordered that every Jew provide a list of his assets under an oath. Alas, after counting the entire Jewish assets and selling even all the Keleh Kodesh, (precious sacramental objects) from all the Prague synagogues, the community only came up with a quarter of the demanded money. To get an idea of what an immense sum the king demanded, it will suffice to say that in 1417 the whole town of Luzice was sold by the emperor to the Teutonic Order for sixty-three thousand golden ducats. Only three days were left to do something. Another merciless and exhausting night came. The Meshores (servants) had already lit modest lights in the community town hall. No hope was in sight. Some suggested turning for help to richer and larger Jewish communities in the German Empire. Little did they know of geography—before the time their messenger would reach the borders, the day of horror would arrive.

Finally, someone came up with an idea that they should see the king and appeal for his mercy, or at least for a postponement of the ultimatum. However, what seemed a reasonable suggestion was practically impossible to do. Under heavy penalties, it was then strictly forbidden for any Jew to cross the limits of the Prague Royal Castle. Even though there were many courageous men in the community, who would dare to enter a lion's den to wrest the spoils from a lion's claws? King Wenceslaus IV was infamous for his fury. He was known to have set his fierce dogs on people from his close circle. The dogs tore them to shreds, and the king was not bothered by his victims' mortal screams.

Where to find a man who would make such a great and perhaps futile sacrifice? Who would be capable of such heroism? It was hardly surprising that only a grave silence followed this suggestion. Lo and behold, a lanky figure rose from a dark corner of the town hall and spoke in a powerful voice, "I will!"

More silence followed. The mayor himself was rendered speechless by the man's bravery. When he recovered his voice, the mayor said, "Come closer and tell us in what way do you propose to undertake such a brave deed?"

A skinny and scantily clad man stepped forth. He was well known in the Prague ghetto, a German-born man by the name of Schmuel. He was a trader, and he was called honourably Reb Schmuel-Spacek in the Kehille (community). He earned his living by working

34

mostly in German commercial communities of Bohemia. He never became rich but was able to attain an education that was rare in those times.

Reb Schmuel was also a sought-after speaker. When a legal conflict threatened to break out anywhere, he was called upon to mediate an agreement that was satisfactory to the parties concerned. He even prevented many conflicts between his rich coreligionists and the powerful of the kingdom. In addition, he was often asked to act as an arbiter in business disputes within the German commercial community. What was special about this man was that he never accepted a single groschen for his time and service.

This was the man who stepped before the mayor. To answer the mayor's inquiry, he only replied, "Mekhas (Your Excellency), please do not disturb my plan, and leave this to the Almighty and me.

"I only have one favour to ask you. I am a poor man and the father of a family. Should I succeed in my mission and fall its victim, then please look after my loved ones. Should I fail in the mission entirely, then the Almighty, who protects widows and orphans, will surely take mercy upon my dear wife and children."

"You, my dear sir," and here he turned to an old Rav (rabbi), "I beg you to pray to the Lord and our Creator that he lends me his merciful protection and help."

Reb Schmuel was promised both, and long after

midnight, the members of the assembly went home. Reb Schmuel walked slowly back to his dwelling in the old school quarter. His mind was racing; he was thinking of what awaited him at home—he would have to break the news to his wife. His feet became very heavy. What is he to tell her? Compared with telling his wife of tomorrow's mission, the mission itself seemed suddenly easy.

His poor wife sat home by a meagre light, waiting for her husband's return. Welcoming him back, she served him a dinner.

Reb Schmuel did not eat much. With his heart beating loudly enough to hear, he rose from the dining table to tell his wife about the council meeting and his decision. First, she listened without uttering a sound as he explained the dilemma. However, when he spoke of his task for the next day, she broke into sobs. Crying, she threw herself on the floor. She embraced her husband's knees and begged him to change his terrible decision. Reb Schmuel tried to console his wife with loving words, but he would not change his mind.

His desperate wife now woke their children from deep sleep, crying that they pray to the Lord that their father would not give himself for the others and make her a widow and the children orphans. Reb Schmuel fought his bitter tears. He loved and adored his family, but not for one moment did he waiver in his decision. He then informed them about how he had looked after their future. This, his wife and children heard while crying.

At last, Reb Schmuel asked them to leave him in peace in his study so that he could find courage and deliberate for the next day's task. After he embraced and blessed everyone for the last time, he retired to bed in his tiny bedroom to catch at least some rest.

* * *

Too soon, the dawn arrived. As soon as the first sun lit the Prague spires with its golden rays, the servants knocked on people's doors, waking them up and telling them the rabbi's order. Whether they were young or old, hungry or full, they were to go to their synagogue and pray for Reb Schmuel's success.

Schmuel was up early; he dressed in old but clean and festive attire and left home quietly, so as not to wake up and upset his family with more farewells.

He walked slowly and entered the cemetery; he stood before the tomb of his parents in a silent prayer and meditation until the Old Town Clock struck eight o'clock in the morning. Having gathered courage, he went to meet his fate. He left the Jewish Town through a small back gate in the place where the Rudolfinum, a concert hall, stands today. Reb Schmuel then walked on the Charles Bridge, approaching Mala Strana, toward the Prague Castle.

* * *

In those unhappy times, there were two men who wielded much influence in the circle of King Wenceslaus IV. Although the king was very difficult to approach and hated to be influenced by anyone, he occasionally listened to these men's advice. One of these men was Wratislaus of Rosenberg, the Lord Huntsmaster of the Kingdom. He was a man of great abilities and acumen, who often stood at the king's side in the most dangerous undertakings. While he displayed courage that bordered on insanity, he lacked sensitivity and rarely used his power to any good ends. Wratislaus also shared all the king's eccentricities, and he was his companion in hunting.

The other man was Lord Pankreas of Hradec, the Lord Chancellor of Bohemia. This aging man, whose hair had greyed in the service of the previous great Luxembourg, was a true nobleman. The only reason he remained in the service of the wild and impetuous king was that Pankreas promised the king's late father Charles IV that he would do so.

Now and again, Lord Pankreas was able to keep Wenceslaus IV from dangerous acts. Counting on Lord Pankreas's help, Reb Schmuel came up with a plan to approach the king. The plan was conceived while he pondered in bed the night before. Some time ago, Reb

Schmuel had won Pankreas's favour.

This is what happened: The Lord of Hradec was a man wealthy in both land and money. Once he entrusted a vast sum of money to a merchant by the name of van der Gracht, an expatriate Dutchman who lived in Prague. He asked van der Gracht to invest the money and keep it out of the king's sight. This business relationship lasted for years. The Dutchman always reaped a lion's share of the profit, but the chancellor was still satisfied. His investment was well hidden, and he saw a small profit as a better option than exposing his money to the king's greed.

As anti-German sentiment grew in the Kingdom of Bohemia, foreign merchants were beginning to leave Prague, and they moved their businesses to Poland. Van der Gracht tried to take advantage of the situation. Pretending an intention to move to Poland, he planned to collect all his claims and then to flee to England with the chancellor's money. He succeeded in sending some of it to England.

Through business contacts, Reb Schmuel found out about the Dutchman's scheme. He immediately informed the chancellor. The chancellor sent his men to watch van der Gracht, and they soon arrested him while he was trying to flee Prague at night. Much of the stolen money was found on him. The angry chancellor ordered that van der Gracht be publicly flogged and then expelled from the kingdom.

The Lord of Hradec wished to reward Reb Schmuel. The latter, however, stuck to his principles and refused to take a single groschen. The chancellor was shocked—until then he had imagined every Jew was greed itself. Instead, Reb Schmuel asked the chancellor for a favour in the future. This, the awed nobleman promised.

So now, Reb Schmuel was on his way to ask for his favour. Right-away, he was admitted to the chancellor's palace, where everyone knew him, and he was shown to an audience hall. The large room was already crowded with people waiting to see the powerful chancellor, from dukes and bishops to common peasants.

Reb Schmuel took his seat in a corner at the end of the line to wait for his turn. Long minutes passed, and it seemed that the waiting crowd was becoming larger. Schmuel began to feel great worries—if the chancellor did not see him today, the deadline would expire, and all would be lost! He was about to resign—let the Almighty's will be done.

Suddenly, the door to the chancellor's office opened, and out came two men. One of them was the chancellor. He looked at the crowd and right-away noticed Reb Schmuel. He beckoned to him, and after his lieutenant informed everyone else present that there would be no more audiences today, he asked Reb Schmuel to follow him into his office.

Barely had Reb Schmuel bowed respectfully, when the chancellor spoke, "I am truly glad to see you, Schmuel! Perhaps, I might be able to repay your favour at last. So, tell me what brings you here? Make it short, though, for I'm on my way to see the king."

"That's just it, My Lord, I must see the king, too," said Reb Schmuel and began to explain to the chancellor the reasons for his request.

The chancellor's face turned red; he rose and shouted, "Are you out of your mind? Don't you know that Jews are forbidden to even step beyond the Castle limits? Still, you are asking me to take you straight to the king! What trouble gives you the courage to ask me to fall into the king's disgrace?"

Reb Schmuel was not one to be frightened by the furious words. He begged the chancellor to listen. The fate of thousands of people depended on it. The fuming chancellor listened. Strange emotions were boiling within him. His nobleman's pride told him to keep his promise. The Jew standing before him was, in his simple bravery, beginning to resemble the ancient Greek heroes or those of patrician Rome. Here was a man who did not hesitate to risk his life for his people. Nevertheless, how could the chancellor take part in such a perilous mission?

Using a milder tone, the chancellor then tried to explain to Schmuel that such a deed would surely be futile. "You really don't know our king. You have no idea what he is capable of in his fury. Go back while you can; there is no point in risking your life in vain. Believe me, not even I can help your people. Once the king has something in his mind, there is no way anyone can change that. And you want to do that with speaking? You will be dead before you can say four words!"

Like lightning, an idea went through Schmuel's head. That was it! That was just the joke that might appeal to king's taste, perhaps a deadly one, one with a bloody point, but one that was worth the try. He explained the idea to the chancellor—he would say only four words to the king.

This time the chancellor listened with patience. He felt sorry for the Jew, who would probably lose his life that very day. However, if Schmuel would not have it otherwise, then so be it.

"Very well, then," the chancellor said. "But remember, Schmuel, if you say more than those four words without the king's explicit order, it will probably be the end of you."

"I am prepared for that, My Lord," replied Schmuel.

The chancellor thought hard but fast. "Hold onto the board of my carriage that will be travelling to the Castle. The servants will be ordered to leave you alone. Once we arrive at the Castle, follow me and wait at the entrance of the room that I enter. Then, I should shortly come out in the king's entourage. This will be your chance to speak to him. Pray to God that you can leave the Castle alive and well."

Reb Schmuel nodded and bowed in agreement.

* * *

The chancellor's carriage rushed to the Prague Castle. Reb Schmuel waited by the door the chancellor had entered. He was praying Shemah Israel (Hear O Israel) to heaven when the door flew opened.

King Wenceslaus IV appeared followed by terrifying dogs, his inseparable companions. The king, whose face was not endowed by any features that would inspire confidence to begin with, bore an especially cruel expression that day. His was the face of a tiger ready to pounce on its victim. The most disconcerting feature of his face was a malicious smile that hovered in a crooked corner of his mouth.

The king stopped before Reb Schmuel and spoke to him in an icy, mocking tone, "So you are the miserable Prague Jew who dares to enter here despite my orders? You must be a great orator if you want to convince me of your case with a mere four words. Speak then and remember that if I hear one more syllable than those four words, you'll end up in the executioner's hands."

Reb Schmuel knew that the king would follow through with his threat. It was known that Master Jan, the Castle Executioner, was one of the king's favourite drinking pals. Many a night, they stayed up drinking, perhaps even all last night. The executioner was always near the king.

If Reb Schmuel was frightened, he did not show it—not a muscle in his face moved; he did not pale. He stepped closer to the king, looked him in the eye, and said, "Vayoumer Adonai el Soton."

The amazed king said, "What's that? What's that supposed to mean?"

Reb Schmuel only pointed his hand to his silent mouth.

"Speak, miserable Jew, I order you!" commanded the king.

"Well," Shmuel said, "if Your Majesty orders, then I must obey. These four words are in Hebrew and they mean 'The Eternal spoke to Satan.' If Your Majesty does not believe me, men of the New Faith can be sent for. They know our holy language well. They will surely confirm the correctness of my translation."

Schmuel went on courageously. "And what is all that supposed to mean?

"It says that God, who has always been here and will continue to be here for eternity, spoke to Satan. He, the highest power in the universe, spoke to his most despised creation. And you, who are certainly one of the most powerful men of the world, German Emperor and Czech

44

King, are still a mortal who one day will turn to ashes. But you don't want to hear out another man, even if he is just a miserable Jew. That's what it is supposed to mean."

The king was speechless. Two powers fought each other in his chest. His rage at the audacity of the Jew's words—never had anyone dared to speak to him like that—told him to punish the Jew by throwing him to his killer dogs. Yet, the king was deeply impressed by the man's bravery. A few moments of dreadful silence passed. The Lord of Hradec, deathly pale, trembled and had to hold on to the doorframe not to faint. Schmuel kept his posture, while the king's face betrayed signs of his internal struggle.

At last, the king interrupted the silence. This time, the noble spirit won in his mind and heart. "So," he spoke to Schmuel in an abrupt but calm voice, devoid of the previous contempt, "tell me your request."

Only now did Schmuel throw himself at the king's feet. He spoke to the king, using words which magically came from one heart to find their way to another. He told the king of the suffering of his people and about what caused it. He shared with the king all they had done to satisfy the king's will, and he appealed to the king's justice. Feeling tired, he paused in his speech.

The king thundered, "Enough! Rise and hear my decision!"

When King Wenceslaus IV did not suffer from fits of rage, which was not often, he was capable of just deeds. He was convinced of the truthfulness of the Jew's words. He said, "This time your payment is waived," and speaking to the chancellor, "We will have to find that money elsewhere."

Reb Schmuel fell on his knees before the king again and thanked him. He barely spoke a few words, when the king ordered, "Rise, Schmuel! I want no thanks. Instead, ask for a favour for yourself."

Being true to his principles even in this moment, Reb Schmuel answered, "Your Majesty, you have just granted me the greatest of favours, and therefore I ask for no more."

This time, however, the good Reb Schmuel was to reap a reward for his courage and modesty. The king said, "You deserve great recognition for your bravery. No one in the world can say that King Wenceslaus leaves heroic men unrewarded. From now on, you are a Royal Court Jew. You may enter all my castles and palaces without any hindrance at any time. But wait!" the king continued. "What's your name?"

"Schmuel, Your Majesty."

"That's right, you Jews have no family names," replied the king. "You must have one then."

Once again, a malicious smile appeared on the king's lips. "You also need to be punished for the audacity of

46

speaking to your king. From this day, you and your descendants will bear the family name of Satan."

The audience was over. Reb Schmuel went happily back home as Schmuel Satan. He received a happy welcome there.

Reb Schmuel's family indeed bore the family name of Satan for the following three hundred years. At last, the family became extinct by the death of Reb Moshe Satan.

8. An Unfortunate Deal

Behind the Church of St. Cosmas and Damian is a courtyard of the famous Emmaus Monastery. Opposite the main church entrance is an old, boarded up monastery staircase, no longer in use due to its poor state. The staircase is said to be haunted by the ghost of a monk. Many residents of Podskali have seen him there. He appears suddenly before the entrance or on the wooden stairs. While some see him headless, others see him with his head on. However, all the eyewitnesses claim that the monk always jingles a bag full of ducats.

The ghost belongs to an Emmaus Monastery monk who had not liked the monastery-regimented life and who planned to flee and to start a new life. For that, he needed much money. In that, he had devilish luck. He heard of a Prague Jew who desired the Holy Host. The Jew believed that he could use the Holy Host for magic against his enemies. Therefore, the monk and the Jew struck a bargain—they would meet on the wooden stairs, where the monk would trade the Holy Host for a bag of ducats with the Jew. The Jew would also bring him civilian clothes, so that the monk could leave the monastery for good. Back then, the wooden staircase was already boarded up, and this became fatal for both parties of the deal. The staircase was locked at night. Locking it was one of the monk's duties. At the regular time, he locked the staircase upper door and went to meet his business partner downstairs.

The Jew was waiting for the monk already. They both entered the staircase interior, and the monk locked the downstairs door as well. This was so that they could realize their deal without witnesses. However, God decided otherwise. Another monk was busy in the monastery garden near the wooden staircase. Suddenly, he heard strange talking inside the staircase. He looked in the staircase through a crevice in the lumber and saw one of his monk brothers with a Jew. He further saw the monk giving the Jew the Holy Host in exchange for a bag of ducats.

Immediately, the witnessing monk ran to tell his brothers. All happened in a very short moment. Before the deal was done, a group of monks rushed to the staircase and surprised the two sinners red-handed. They were both handed to city guards and charged with sacrilege. As sacrilege was a capital crime, their trial was speedy and their sentences cruel. The Jew was quartered and burned at the stake. The monk was beheaded in the place his crime occurred, on the monastery stairs. Secular justice was thus served.

However, on Good Friday, commemorating the day when Jesus Christ died on the cross for humankind, the headless monk appeared on the monastery stairs, holding his head under one arm and a bag of ducats in another. His ghost cried and lamented. The Jew did not find peace after his death either. His ghost was seen on the staircase arguing with the headless monk.

The unfortunate monk is still waiting for his absolution, which can only be delivered by a newly consecrated priest. In the first night of his office, the priest can free the monk-ghost from eternal condemnation if he administers the headless monk the Holy Host and takes the bag of ducats from him. No one has yet dared to do such a brave deed.

The Emmaus monks built a new stone staircase by the Church of St. Kosmas and Damian, but they did not tear down the old wooden staircase. This, they believed, was to allow the unfortunate monk to be freed from his predicament. Otherwise, the famous monastery would be afflicted by a great misfortune.

In the Cathedral of St. Vitus, there is an ambit of fifteen arched sections with thirteen adjacent chapels. Next to the Pernstejn Chapel is the Chapel of John the Baptist, also called the Chapel of St. Anthony the Hermit or the Arnost Chapel, which was built by Arnost of Pardubice, the Archbishop of Prague, at his expense in 1352. A sacral object called the Candelabra of Jerusalem can be found in this chapel.

According to an old legend, the candelabra was first brought to the city of Milan by the Roman Emperor Titus from Solomon's Temple.

The candelabra's bronze under-part is a rare antique, which is said to have been taken to Prague from Milan by Czech warriors after they had conquered Milan as allies of the German Emperor Friedrich I the Red-Beard. The oldest Czech account of this is given by chronicler Dalimil, "In the Castle, in St. Vitus Cathedral, stands the foot of a Candelabra of Solomon. It was taken from Jerusalem by the Mediolanenes, who, along with Titus and Vespecianus, fought the Jews. If you wish, you can see the candelabra foot before the altar."

As early as the 13th century, the candelabra was believed to be ancient. In 1359 the candelabra was put on a white marble pedestal with an engraving saying, "This is the Candelabra of Solomon's Temple in Jerusalem, acquired by the Duke and the Czech lords in Milan, and installed here in 1395 A.D."

According to experts, the candelabra comes from the eighth or ninth century A.D. It stands upon bizarre animal heads and claws and consists of various monsters, dragons, and human figures. The candelabra's multi-shouldered top, with busts of Czech patron saints, was made on the behest of Archduke Leopold Wilhelm, the Bishop of Bratislava, in 1641. A plaque above confirms this.

10. THE PINKAS SYNAGOGUE

In the street of Siroka of the Prague Jewish Town of Josefov stands an old building known as the Pinkas Synagogue. Today the synagogue stands somewhat under street level. This is because the Vltava riverbank was artificially raised in the beginning of the 20th century. Inside of the synagogue is a sad reminder of that very century. Its walls are covered by the names of eighty thousand Czech and Moravian Jews who perished in the Holocaust of World War II.

Despite many visitors year-round, the Pinkas Synagogue gives a quiet, dreamy impression. Perhaps the synagogue beckons to those who dream their eternal dreams in the adjacent Old Jewish Cemetery. The Pinkas Synagogue was founded as early as in the 15th century. It was enlarged in the 17th century and rebuilt again in 1862.

Here is the legend that tells about the founding of the Pinkas Synagogue. More than four hundred years ago, a man by the name of Pinkas lived in the Prague Jewish Town. He was a poor, hardworking man, honest to the last fibre of his body. During the day, he walked in the streets and bought used clothing to sell in his shop. At night, he sat in his small room and studied Halakha

(Jewish religious law) at a dimly lit lamp.

Pinkas was rarely able to make enough money to provide for his family. He would have possibly died from hunger, along with his wife and children, if it were not for one wealthy and kind-hearted count who liked Pinkas for his honesty and piety and helped him with money. Every Friday, Pinkas saw his patron and gave him a detailed accounting of the last week's earnings and expenses. If Pinkas did not have enough money left to be able to celebrate Sabbath as prescribed by Jewish laws, the count reached into his pocket and covered what lacked.

Pinkas was thankful to his patron, but his pious mind saw the count as an angel sent by God and his charity as a gift by the Almighty. The way he thanked the count was more of a prayer than recognition. Every time Pinkas received his donation, he raised his eyes toward heaven and said, "Thank you God, who doesn't abandon your children in times of need; thank you for helping me again." This bothered the count.

After the holidays, the count asked the good Pinkas if he enjoyed them. Pinkas always said that God helped him and never acknowledged the count for his help. Finally, the count had enough of Pinkas's "ungratefulness." He thought to himself, "What gratitude! I'm helping the Jew so that he can celebrate his Sabbath, and he's thanking God for help. I'm highly curious how he proposes to get on with the next holiday if I withhold my generosity. Let's see how much his God helps him then."

Such an opportunity arrived with the coming of Pesah (Passover), a Jewish holiday celebrating the flight of Jews from Egyptian slavery. A few days before Passover, every Jew, rich or poor, must have food for eight days. According to the Jewish law of Talmud, everyone must drink four cups of wine with bread on the first two evenings. Yes, even the beggars. So as usual before the holidays, Pinkas went to see the count for money. However, this time the count did not smile when Pinkas approached him.

After hearing Pinkas tell him about the upcoming holidays, the count said, "My dear Pinkas, this time you will have to provide your own bread. I'm in financial trouble. The rent from my properties hasn't arrived, and I've had many great expenses. But I'm sure your God will help you since you always thank him so nicely."

Indeed, Pinkas's emaciated face was beset with worry. Still, the unshakable faith of his ancestors had not left him. He only heaved his shoulders and said sadly, "What is there to do? God will help!" Pinkas went home in gloom.

At home, his wife waited for him in anticipation. His children, who looked forward to promised gifts, showered Pinkas with questions. "How much did you get this year?" his wife asked and stretched out her palm.

"How much did I get?" answered Pinkas. "Nothing, that's what I got." He threw his empty bag into a corner and went to prepare for his evening prayer.

His wife would not have that for an answer and began to complain loudly. The children cried from hunger, and the wife would not stop berating him. Pinkas was in anguish. Silently, he went to his study, shut the door, and as always, read Jewish scripts until Midnight.

The children were sleeping on their thin hay mattresses, and even the wife fell asleep, while crying that her husband was not even able to provide for his own family. Pinkas sat at his desk, stroking his beard and thinking. He could not concentrate.

Suddenly, someone smashed the study window from the outside. A frightful figure flew in, hit the floor, and collapsed at Pinkas's feet. He jumped up in horror and held his thick book in front of him as a shield. Outside, a screeching laughter of more voices sounded, as if a pack of Massikins (evil spirits) were there to harm him. Pinkas gathered his courage and looked at the human-like figure on the floor. He took an oil lamp off his desk and looked closer.

That the monster on the floor was a dead monkey did not add to Pinkas's calm. He knew that wealthy people kept monkeys as pets, but he thought of monkeys as being half-human. He also knew that such a monkey had great value. Now Pinkas was truly scared. Recalling all the tragic events of the recent years, he mumbled to himself, "Now they will come again to kill me and my brothers, to annihilate us from the face of the earth. They will accuse me of killing the monkey. God have mercy on an innocent man!" he cried.

His wife, woken by the ruckus, burst through the door and inquired what had happened. Pinkas told her, and she cried, "Yes, they want to destroy us; this is a trap. We must get rid of the animal."

"But how do we do that?" asked Pinkas. "Should I wrap up the body and dump it in the river? I could fall into the hands of city guards—such a burden would look suspicious. Also, I'm not sure if I could carry it myself."

They thought about it for a while until Pinkas exclaimed, "I know what to do! We will burn it." Therefore, Mrs. Pinkas started a strong fire in the kitchen oven. Pinkas and his wife then grabbed the dead monkey by its feet. They were about to drag it in the kitchen, when a shiny object fell out of the monkey's mouth. They both dropped the body. A golden ducat shone on the floor.

Pinkas lifted the body off the floor. It seemed heavier than he would expect it to be. He felt the dead monkey's belly. Grabbing a kitchen knife, he cut the belly open. He took out the stomach and opened it. Lo and behold, it was full of golden ducats. Pinkas rejoiced and raised his eyes to heaven in a religious fervour, "I was young, and I grew old. I have never seen a pious man abandoned and his children go hungry."

Mrs. Pinkas's face lit with joy. Right-away, they picked up the ducats. It was a handsome pile. They cut up the monkey's carcass, burned it in the oven, and washed the blood off the floor.

Their task was finished before dawn—not a hair was left from the dead monkey, and the ducats were safely put away.

"What you give to the sacred holidays, the Lord pays you back many times!" says the Talmud, so Pinkas gave his wife what she asked for the holidays. New clothes for the children were purchased, along with new white wash, gold embroidered hats, and other luxuries. In addition, they bought much meat and wine. Perhaps never before was the Pinkas' household as happy and festive as on that day. Only the day before poverty reigned; now there was joy and plenty. Never did the Pinkases celebrate the Eve of Passover with such happiness and piety.

The family gathered at the table. Mrs. Pinkas was dressed in a long, white Schpenzer and a gold-embroidered veil richly decorated with wide lace ribbons and fringes. She filled the glasses with wine. The children sat at the table, their faces full of joy, expecting things that were to come. As prescribed, on the table stood a round-shaped tin vessel with three pieces of Matzoth, unleavened bread, wrapped in a large cloth. This was in the memory of the Jewish escape from slavery in Egypt. When the Jews fled, they did not have time to leaven their bread. On the top of the cloth were horseradish, boiled eggs, a piece of roasted meat, and a small dish of salty water. Together the family lifted the tin vessel, reciting the verse, "This is the bread of poverty, which our fathers ate in the country of Misraim. Enter whoever is hungry and eat with us."

They had barely finished when a carriage rumbled outside. There was a violent knocking on the door. Pinkas, pale with apprehension, ran to the door, "Who is it?"

"Just open the door, dear Pinkas. I'm here to celebrate your Pesach with you," the count's voice answered. At first, all gathered thought that it was Elijah the Prophet himself who visits every pious Jew at that time. A special glass must always be prepared for him on the table.

Pinkas opened the door and bowed to his patron.

"Please don't be bothered by my presence," the count said. "But what do I see?" he exclaimed in surprise, looking at the room. "Is this still your house, Pinkas? Or have you become rich?"

"Yes, I have," Pinkas replied. "The Almighty helped me. Only a few days ago I was poor, and I didn't even know how I could celebrate the holidays as true Jews should. However, like the old saying goes, 'When the need is high, God's help is close.' Now I am a rich man."

"Would you care to tell me about it?" asked the count.

"Of course," replied Pinkas and began telling the amazed count what had happened.

As soon as he mentioned the dead monkey, the count interrupted him, "What? A dead monkey? I lost one a few days ago. What did you do with it?"

Pinkas shared with the count more details. Describing the monkey, he added that the animal had a red collar around its neck. The count said, "That was, no doubt, my monkey, then." Still, he could not fathom how the monkey ended in Pinkas's study. Now Pinkas went to his bedroom, came back with a bag of ducats, and handed it to the count, "Here is what is yours, except for a couple of ducats we used for the holidays."

"What about the bag?" the count asked.

Here, Pinkas told the count the rest of the story. He said that he thought it had been help from God. An explanation of the mystery was beginning to dawn on the count. He was in the habit of testing the veracity of golden coins by biting into them with his teeth. The monkey must have copied this behaviour and swallowed the coins for real. That was the end of the poor animal.

The count turned to the servant who accompanied him and stood nearby, "Do you know about this?"

"I beg your forgiveness, My Lord," he answered, shaking. "Our footman wanted to play a little joke on Pinkas, so he threw the dead monkey into his window. A few other servants knew."

"Hmm," the count said, "So, I had the footman put behind bars, and he hadn't sold or killed the monkey after all. But he still needs to be punished for the crime he committed against poor Pinkas here."

"Here is the gold," said Pinkas, handing the bag to the count again.

"No, dear Pinkas, I don't want it back," the count said. "This year I didn't give you anything. I wanted to know if your God would indeed help you because that's what you always say. Now I see that your confidence in God was justified. It was He who sent you the money. Tonight, I wish to share your joy with you. Therefore, dear Pinkas, please go on with the celebration. Only let me send for my wife so that she can join us, too."

Soon, the countess arrived and was in no less awe after she had heard the story. The count and countess only left after the Seder (feast) was over and Pinkas finished it with the verse, "One day God shall destroy the Angel of Death."

* * *

In a few years, with the count's money, Pinkas

61

gained great wealth through his diligence and wisdom. He was well respected among his coreligionists and was elected a Parnas (mayor). Despite all that, he remained an honest and humble man. His house was a centre of learned rabbis; his hand was always open for those needing help; his table hosted the hungry daily. No one ever left empty-handed.

On the street where Pinkas lived, he built many homes for the poor in addition to a beautiful synagogue. Pinkas lived to see an old age. His famous synagogue is called the Pinkas Synagogue to this very day.

11. THE PRAGUE EASTER POGROM

Grave silence descended upon the Jewish Town of Prague. The streets of the town were deserted. A bloody struggle had just raged there, and the streets were strewn with thousands of bodies of Jewish men, boys, girls, and even mothers with babies. Only the victorious cries of the cruel enemy sounded in the distance.

Three shade-like figures leaned over the dead whose souls had already bid farewell to their bodies. "I have faith," said the first of the figures, "that the days of the dwellers of the Jewish Town of Prague are not numbered yet."

"I will do what I can and save them! It is not the Lord's will that the town should perish!" said the second figure.

"Such is your faith, and I will help you in your effort!" said the third figure.

They stopped the bleeding of those who still lived and took them to safety. Then, with care only Love can give, they cared for the wounded. Many of those who were dying lived, thanks to their saviours—Faith, Hope, and Love. Left by the Eternal and persecuted by fate, Jews were being murdered, falling into a certain grave. Yet, He who runs fates of people and rules the nations decided otherwise.

This tragedy took place within the walls of the Jewish Town of Prague on Easter, April 18, 1389, during the reign of King Wenceslaus IV. Eternal blame rests upon the ruler who, in his aloofness or incompetence, failed to prevent this tragedy and let the murderers escape without just punishment.

The crime was committed by an agitated mob that murdered and robbed in the Jewish Town under the disguise of religion. The fact that this happened at Easter shows the true disrespect of the perpetrators to the memory of Jesus Christ.

This is what happened: In the afternoon of that tragic day, a Catholic priest was carrying the sacrament of unction to a dying Christian. When he walked by the Jewish Town, he was hit by a piece of clay or sand. It is not known whether the local children did that on purpose or just during playing. The priest's companion began to punish the children despite loud protests of their parents. A street riot broke out, and a few participants were taken to the nearby Old Town jail.

The same evening, a horrible rumour of an offense against a Catholic priest and the Christian religion spread around Prague. An emotion of revenge began boiling among the population. The Old Town Hall tried to quell the unrest and sent city guards into the streets to prevent violence. Then, a fanatic preacher accused the

Old Town Council of protecting the sacrilegious Jews and called for revenge in the name of Jesus Christ.

An insane mob attacked the Jewish Town. They murdered, burned, and looted, while no one was able to do anything. The Prague ghetto fell, and rivers of Jewish blood were spilled. Only a very few saved their lives. Almost four thousand bodies lay in the streets of the Jewish Town of Prague. Any Jew who would not go through forced baptism was killed on the spot. Many Jews ran to the Old New Synagogue and hid there. The attackers broke down the door and murdered everyone inside. During the murders of Jews, many Christian bills of debt were stolen from Jewish hands.

Abigdor Kara, a famous Prague rabbi and a poet, the son of Yitzchak, witnessed the Easter Prague Pogrom as a young man. He left an account of the tragedy in his famous Selicha (Forgiveness). According to his account, the murderous mob burst even into the Old Jewish Cemetery, ripping corpses out of their graves and destroying tombs.

Even though King Wenceslaus IV learned of the mass murder of Prague Jews, he remained indifferent, and according to several Prague historians, did not prosecute the murderers. Only when the murderers fled to Germany, did the king send a small party of horse riders after them. It was too late, and no one was arrested. The king never initiated an investigation of the incident either. The Jews, his most heavily taxed subjects, were left alone in this injustice.

Only Faith, Hope, and Love, the three helping spirits, raised the Jews from ashes and guided them through sad and difficult times. Abigdor Kara died on Saturday, April 25, 1439. He was buried in the Old Jewish Cemetery of Prague.

12. THE MAHARAL OF PRAGUE

Yehudah Löw ben Bezalel, the son of Bezalel, who was the son of Chaim, was a learned Prague Talmudist and Cabalist. He was known as the Eminent Rabbi Löw and the Maharal of Prague. Maharal is an acronym from Moreinu ha-Rav Loewe (Our Teacher the Rabbi Löw, in Hebrew). He was considered a great scholar by both the Jews and Gentiles of Prague.

Rabbi Löw was the Supreme Rabbi and School Rector of Moravia between 1553 and 1537. Later he moved to Prague. In Prague, he spent eleven years before becoming the renowned Rector of the Talmud School founded by him at the Klaus Synagogue. Between the years 1584 and 1573, he was most likely in the Polish city of Poznań. On Sunday of February 16, 1592, Rabbi Löw was summoned to the Prague Castle by Emperor Rudolf II. The emperor always appreciated his company. Together, the two learned men discussed many things, many of which remain secret.

In April of 1592, Rabbi Löw returned to Poznań to hold the office of the School Rector and Supreme Rabbi of the Polish Empire. When he came back to Prague, he became the Supreme Rabbi, which office he held until his death on August 22, 1609.

Rabbi Löw ben Bezalel had done a lot for the Jewish congregation of Prague. He founded a burial society in 1564 and introduced Chevrath ha-Mishnayoth, societies for the organized study of Mishnah (an important section of Talmud). The names of all his famous fifteen works are inscribed on his tombstone.

The people saw a great magician in him. Several legends were told about the Maharal of Prague. Rabbi Löw lived in the street of Siroka in a simple small house where building Number 911 stands today. His house entrance bore an emblem of a lion, the same lion that can be seen on his tombstone. He educated hundreds of excellent pupils.

According to historian Jost, Löw Bezalel lived to be a hundred and four years of age. Some sources give Cracow, Poland, as the place of his last rest. However, a rabbi of the same name who died in 1671 is buried in Cracow, hence the confusion. Still, others claim that he is buried in Poznań, Poland.

However, he was buried in the Old Jewish Cemetery of Prague, where he rests to this day. His wife Perl, daughter of Samuel, died nine months after her husband's death and rests by his side. Löw Bezalel and his wife dream their eternal dreams in the Old Town Jewish Cemetery of Prague, in an oasis of peace in the bustling Czech capital.

13. Golem

The hands of both clocks on the Jewish Town Hall of Prague had already reached noon, and as the clocks struck the time, Rabbi Ezekiel Löw, the first elder of the Jewish community, still had much to take care of. Calling on Mr. Wentura Sax was not a particularly pleasant task, but one that the community had urgently asked him to do. It concerned the very painful fact that in those days many young Prague Jews had begun to abandon the Faith of Moses and convert to Christianity. Just in the last months, four such cases had been reported.

Mr. Sax, a community elder, wanted to discuss yet another such case with Rabbi Löw; Joachim the son of Solomon of the Golden Bell announced his coming baptism. In vain, did his father Solomon, lament, beg, and curse his son as Korach, Dathan, and Abiron. Joachim persisted in his determination to become a Christian and secretly met with his mentors. The circumstances were strong to convert him from the religion of his fathers.

The Vicar of St. John introduced the future Christian to Court Vicar Jan, who was an able speaker and thinker. He soon convinced Joachim to go against his parents' wishes and to give up the Jewish faith for good.

Joachim's parents had no clue where his new conviction came from. First, they believed that their son had fallen victim to black magic. Then, old Solomon followed his son and found out where his son kept going. It was a humble pub in the residence of the Bishop of Vienna in Royal Hradcany. There, Joachim met Master Jost and Father Jan, the Royal Chaplain and Vicar of St. Jacob. He listened to them carefully and nodded.

Little did these gentlemen know what was occupying Joachim's mind. He was in love with a young and beautiful girl, Dorota Profet. It was because of her that he wished to become a Goy (gentile). Once the beautiful girl remarked, "You are such a fine and handsome young man, BUT you are a Jew!"

Joachim made up his mind. He would convert to Christianity and then he would ask Dorota for her hand.

Old Solomon told what he had found out to Wentura Sax, who in turn informed the rabbi. The rabbi's silver-haired head drooped heavy with this knowledge. What was he to do?

"Old Solomon would rather sacrifice his son like Isaac did than to allow such shame," Sax finished his report.

"Yes, we are going down," the rabbi said. "Gone are the old days of Jewishness as we knew it in the times of my famous grandfather Bezalel," he sighed. "Well, try to calm Solomon down. Have him send his son to me tomorrow. I hope that Joachim can be returned to the faith of Moses. If he is to be lost, then let him be lost entirely."

Wentura Sax was encouraged by the rabbi's words and left. Rabbi Löw then went home to his house in the street of Siroka in the Jewish Town of Prague. After he had been welcomed by Sara, his foster-daughter, he sat down on his bench, crossed his arms on his chest, and pondered the news. He did not even notice that Sara brought him supper.

Only after she had asked him whether he was not ill, he repeated the Sax's words to her. "So, the old Solomon would rather sacrifice his son like Isaac," she commented.

"And right he is," replied Rabbi Löw. "He is an old faithful. But he cannot fight treachery with honesty," and the rabbi thought to himself, "The Christian Jesuits say that the end justifies the means. Perhaps they are right." How could this motto be put to use here? The dear Faith of Moses must be defended.

The rabbi spent the whole evening studying. The heavy folios that the back room was filled with were, one by one, moved to the study and read. At last, Ezekiel Löw smiled. His sight dwelled in the middle of a page, in an old Chaldean book.

The rabbi then wrote three lines of Hebrew letters from the book on a strip of parchment. As soon as the ink dried, he called Sara to bring a lit lantern.

She did so and followed the rabbi on a spiral staircase to the attic of the ancient house. There, Rabbi Löw unlocked and opened a few doors, which were never used. After he had slowly opened the last door, he looked around the dusty, dark room. Stepping into a corner, he cast the light upon a dusty figure that looked like a sleeping man lying on the floor. The figure had its mouth open; one of its hands supported its head, while the other hand was attached along the body.

When Sara saw the male figure, she cried in fear and ran out of the room. "Come back, silly Sara," the rabbi called after her. "Don't be afraid, it's just a clay figure. Look at him; he has been lying here for ages. The spark has been extinguished from his eyes a long time ago. Look, when I touch him, what a sound he makes."

Indeed, when the rabbi lightly knocked on the figure, the sound of burned clay came from it.

"He must have been resting here for a very long time, the poor thing," said the rabbi. "But I'm sure we can wake him up today." He took out the parchment and a magic card called Shem. He inserted the Shem into the figure's mouth.

"Golem!" the rabbi then commanded in a powerful voice, "Rise!"

The figure of Golem moved. He stretched and rubbed his eyes. After rising from the floor, he looked around and said, "What do you wish of me, my master?"

Sara did not wait throughout the procedure. In her fright, she took off, and her feet clapped down the stairs to the courtyard. Only after a long while, did she gather the courage to come back.

In the hallway on a chest sat Golem, now full of life and clad in decent clothes. "Sara, let me introduce our new servant Golem to you," said Rabbi Löw with a smile.

* * *

The next morning, a pleasant surprise awaited Sara. She slept late, but the kitchen fire blazed away already. Golem had neatly chopped the firewood and started the fire. Sarah only had to prepare the breakfast.

She looked at Golem hesitatingly. He sat on a chest by the fire. Instead of human eyes, two clay eyes rolled in his head. His nose was pointed, and his brown face was shiny as if it was greased with butter. It was made of glazed clay. As soon as the rabbi called him, Golem left the kitchen. He had to obey his master's commands.

Sara was amazed that she was spared much of her usual work by Golem's labour. He did anything he was ordered and did it fast. He took two huge coal crates and was back with coal before Sarah could count to thirty. When he went to fetch water, he brought a whole tub full of water filled to the brim without spilling a drop. When he chopped firewood, the axe flew off the handle. Golem pushed the axe back onto the handle, using only two fingers.

Golem caused even more awe at noon. At that time, young Joachim, the would-be-convert, arrived for his appointment with Rabbi Löw. First, the rabbi and the young man talked quietly. Rabbi Löw tried his best to convince Joachim to adhere to the religion of his fathers. When all his words failed, the otherwise calm rabbi entered into a loud argument with the young man. The argument turned into a shouting match after Joachim had told the rabbi in his face that the Messiah had come already and that the one the Jews expect will be the Anti-Christ and Devil.

Löw slapped the young man in the face, and a fight ensued. When they were in the thickest of it, the rabbi called his Golem. The Golem grabbed Joachim by his midriff with his one hand and squeezed his legs together with the other hand. In a flash, Golem took the surprised young man down the stairs and threw him outside.

* * *

That Friday, a peculiar party walked across the Charles Bridge to Mala Strana and the Royal Hradcany. Ezechiel Löw was flanked by Old Solomon and his wife Rebecca, followed by Wentura Sax and the tall Golem.

Leaning on a heavy stick, Golem struck a conspicuous figure. Because of his brown face, the passers-by took him for a visitor from a faraway land.

On the way, Rebecca talked animatedly with Rabbi Löw, often asking her husband to agree with her ramblings. The rabbi was reticent; only when he could hardly do otherwise, he nodded. Nothing like the previous afternoon had ever happened to him in his ministerial office. If it were not for Golem, who knows what the whole unpleasantness would have led to? His blood was still boiling in his veins when he thought of the audacity of the young dissident, whom he only tried to help with kind words. And to what ends!

Finally, they arrived at the beautiful Dorota Profet's pub upon a hill. The rabbi was astonished to see who sat in there. Even though the pub's arches were freshly whitewashed, the tables immaculately clean, and the floor scrubbed with sand, Rabbi Löw was not impressed by the pub's patrons. Right-away, the rabbi knew that the "Anti-Christ" and "Devil" Joachim spoke of did not originate in the young man's gullible mind. Next to Joachim sat Royal Chaplain Jan, a lanky man in a black cassock, and Master Jost, the chaplain's zealous assistant.

Rabbi Löw remained calm, and together with his company, he sat down at a nearby table and ordered a good lager beer. Since Dorota was slow to serve them,

Golem was ordered to go the cellar with well-sized pitchers to fetch the beer. When young Joachim arrived, the entire company joined their tables.

Shortly, the vicar of St. Jacob showed up, and an intense debate began. Both parties used their best arguments to defend their religion. The discussion stopped when it grew dark, and the company felt hungry.

Old Rebecca wanted fresh eggs, and since the publican did not have them, she volunteered to get them in the neighbourhood. Dorota then wanted to give the eggs to the cook, but Rebecca sent Golem to the kitchen with a message for the cook, "Let our servant prepare them."

When Golem returned from the kitchen with the meal, a new violent argument was raging among the patrons. Since the food needed salt, Rebecca salted Joachim's dish, and Golem brought more salt from the kitchen.

After the dinner, the Jewish visitors left in a hurry. Joachim bid his old parents farewell by a kiss, not suspecting anything untoward. However, in an hour he began suffering from terrible pains. He convulsed in agony and his entire body was severely swollen. A doctor was called in. He performed bloodletting, but the young Jew died in the greatest pains two hours after his parents' departure.

Rabbi Löw, shaken, was late in the synagogue that

evening. He was absent-minded during his sermon, and he was relieved when the choir began singing the enchanting Lecho Dodi (Sabbath evening hymn). Psalm 92 then filled the synagogue. During the ninety-second psalm, Rabbi Löw suddenly remembered Golem, his great grandfather Bezalel's legacy. It was something to remember! He had heard how Golem ran amuck on the eve of Sabbath, as if he were possessed by the devil. Rabbi Löw's great grandfather Bezalel always removed Shem, the magic card, out of Golem's mouth at such times. Golem would collapse on the floor as if dead. Only on Sunday, did Bezalel replace the Shem in Golem's mouth.

After visiting the Hradcany pub with his master, Golem returned home. First, he sat in the kitchen, but after a while, he became very restless. He began jumping around the house, and when Sara laughed at him, he sprung at her and started to kiss her. The more she fought him, the more ferociously he forced himself on her. Only after he had finished with her, did he let the trembling Sara go and run back to the kitchen. There, he threw pieces of furniture out of the window, followed by kitchen equipment and supplies. No one in the world could move faster than Golem!

When there was nothing left in the kitchen, save the stove and fireplace, Golem attacked his absent master's bedroom. In no time, Rabbi Löw's bedroom slippers and his entire wardrobe flew out on the street. The passers-by outside readily welcomed these gifts. Whether Jew or Christian, they were already fighting for the rabbi's fur coat and other articles of exquisite clothing. However, they all dispersed when a heavy armoire almost landed on their heads.

Golem was still far from being done—more and more furniture ended on the street. The crowd in the street of Siroka grew by the minute and loudly cheered Golem, their benefactor. He tossed them whatever he happened to get into his hands. One man received a nice polished table, another received velvet curtains. The women present were collecting fine linens and pillows.

Only several Jews, who were clueless about what was going on, went into the rabbi's house to investigate. There, they only met with Golem's merciless fury. Sara, who by now had gathered her wits, ran out of the house crying.

Fortunately, Rabbi Löw hurried home. Seeing a large crowd and hearing all the noise, he knew not to expect anything good. He rushed into one of his rooms. Golem was just about to "organize" his library.

"What should I do?" the rabbi thought. "By singing the ninety-second psalm, Sabbath began already, and I am not supposed to do anything." He did not have much time for pondering, though. "Take my Sabbath...," he thought, and after a short struggle, he removed the Shem

78

out of Golem's mouth. Golem crumbled on the floor lifeless.

The rabbi then returned to the synagogue and began the Psalm 92 again. Although this struck his congregation as strange, they sang along, and the sin was thus undone. Golem was rendered harmless for good. Late at night, the rabbi forced Sara to help him carry Golem back to the attic quietly. Thus, the perpetrator of the crime in the Hradcany pub was hidden there forever.

The news of the Hradcany murder soon spread throughout the whole town and caused turmoil among Christians. The poisoning of a Christian neophyte by Jews was seen as an inappeasable hatred toward Christianity. Yet, the only truly guilty party was Golem. Young Dorota Profet, the Hradcany publican's daughter, told the authorities that the only person bringing the visitors food and beer that night had indeed been Golem. She was convinced that he was the murderer of Joachim.

While many did not believe her, a warrant of arrest was issued for Golem. He was not to be found. All three remaining Jewish pub patrons were arrested and put in jail for three days. However, since no prosecutor wanted to pursue the case, they were let go.

After Rabbi Löw had returned from the jail, he found a note on his desk written by Royal Chaplain Jan.

"Alas, Golem, your last service missed its purpose!" cried the rabbi bitterly. "He died a Christian."

The note read:

Dear Rabbi Löw,

This is to inform you that Joachim, the son of Solomon, was baptised by me in the sacristy of St. Vitus Cathedral, witnessed by Master Jost and Sexton Razna, by the Christian name of Jiri.

Yours Truly,

Jan, Royal Chaplain

14. STOP PRAYING!

Another legend about Golem tells the following: It happened once that the adolescent daughter of Rabbi Ezekiel Löw fell ill. Her father tried his best to cure her, knowing a few secrets of natural science. This time, however, he failed, for he was not able to recognize the cause of the illness.

The girl grew weaker, and the father, burdened with great worries, sat by her bed, forgetting his synagogue duties. Friday almost reached its eve when a Chazzan (cantor), who usually presented synagogue singing, entered the room and said, "Say, Rabbi, why don't we start early today? It's very hot and the souls in purgatory could use some cooling." The rabbi was too stricken with worries, so he told the cantor to begin the Saturday service without him.

After the cantor had left, the rabbi lit the candles and prayed Cabbala Shabbat (prayer welcoming the coming of Saturday). His daughter Ester whispered her prayer along. When they arrived at the tenth verse, the cantor burst into the room, shaken by fear, and exclaimed, "Rabbi! The Golem!"

Only now did the rabbi recall that he forgot to take the Shem, the magic card, out of Golem's mouth. Unless he did so soon, a tragedy could occur. He put his daughter to bed and rushed to the synagogue.

The congregation was at the first psalm, but they could hardly pray for fear, so their singing sounded more like shouts. Golem ran amuck about the synagogue, destroying anything that came into his way. The arc of the covenant fell; the candleholders were scattered on the floor; the synagogue was dark as if before a great thunderstorm. Rabbi Löw faced the praying and called to them, "Stop praying!"

As soon as they stopped, the power of Golem was broken, because the Sabbath begins only after the singing of the first psalm. The rabbi removed the Shem out of Golem's mouth and inserted another one in its place. Right-away, the fierce brute turned into a servant, tame as a lamb. The Jews lit the candles, praising the wisdom of their minister. They prayed for the recovery of his daughter.

At that moment, the Malach Hamavod (the Angel of Death), who had already been sent by God to the rabbi's house, retreated. The Almighty was moved by the warm prayers of the community and recalled the Angel of Death.

When the rabbi came back home, he found his daughter feeling better. Soon, she recovered entirely. In memory of this event, whenever Psalm 92 is sung in the Old-New Synagogue, it is sung twice.

15. Ben Bezalel and Emperor Rudolf II

When Emperor Rudolf and his famous astronomer, Tycho de Brahe, visited Löw ben Bezalel in his humble house, the Eminent Rabbi conjured up the entire Hradcany Court as if he had moved it there. The emperor was highly impressed and bestowed many honours on the magician.

Once, a strange idea occurred to the emperor. He wished to see Jewish patriarchs and the sons of Jacob. He therefore asked the rabbi to evoke them from the dead. The rabbi agreed and promised the emperor to do so under one condition. No matter what the emperor would see, he was not to laugh. The emperor gave him his promise.

The day and place were given. The patriarchs were to be seen in one of the large rooms of the Royal Castle. Indeed, the Jewish patriarchs appeared one after the other, and the emperor was in awe of the statures and strength of these famous men.

Only when Naphtali, the Fast One, ran through fields of wheat and flax, could the emperor no longer hold himself back and smiled. Suddenly, the magic scene disappeared, and the arch of the room began to descend upon the viewers' heads. The ceiling would have surely buried the emperor and his companions if the rabbi had not stopped it by a magic formula. There is still one room in Prague Castle that is never opened. It is said to have a lowered, fallen arch.

During the reign of Emperor Rudolf II, Prague was a gathering place for the most distinguished men of the times. Among them were the famous astronomers Tycho de Brahe, Johannes Kepler, and Christen Sørensen Longomontanus. The emperor himself was a learned scholar, and his love for science not only attracted a number of scientists and artists from all Europe, but his example also inspired many members of the nobility, who undertook various disciplines of science.

One such nobleman was a wealthy and powerful count living outside of Prague. He stayed out of the noise of the capital and dedicated himself to the studies of astronomy and astrology. He was an enthusiastic fan of Löw ben Bezalel, the Eminent Rabbi of Prague, and often invited the rabbi to stay at his country estate. The rabbi also loved the learned count's company. Together they talked about secret sciences.

One day after a scholarly discussion lasting for hours, and before the rabbi was about to return to Prague, the count said, "Listen, Rabbi, explain one thing to me, though. You have more than four hundred students whom you teach in your house. However, you have but a small house with two rooms. How do you find space for them all?"

"My dear count," answered the rabbi, "I would find enough room for them even if their number doubled or tripled."

"That's difficult to believe," the count remarked.

"I understand," the rabbi replied. "Nevertheless, to prove the truthfulness of my words, I ask for your permission to host you with any number of your friends and staff in my house, while all my students are there in the morning." The count accepted the invitation; the day was set, and the rabbi went back to Prague.

* * *

On the day of the experiment, the count arrived at the rabbi's house. As agreed upon, he brought many of his friends and a few of his servants along. They stepped out of their carriages in front of the house, which struck them as inhospitable with walls blackened by age and smoke. However, after they had entered they could not believe their senses—the house was magnificent and spacious inside. As far as the eye could see, all was built in the finest architecture.

The guests stepped into the hallway and saw a long row of rooms. The count and his friends were bewildered by the sophisticated taste of the rabbi, who until now had, it seemed, paid little attention to worldly things.

The lunch hour struck, and both wings of the dining hall opened. A long table stood in the centre, laden with exquisite dishes. Golden goblets stood next to silver plates full of the most delicious foods. The count and his friends, who often sat at the royal dining table, had to admit to themselves that the rabbi's table could easily match that of the emperor's. The company sat, ate, drank, and entertained themselves in an excellent mood.

During the banquet, the count inconspicuously instructed his butler to take and hide one of the golden goblets. At the end, all guests rose from their seats and left, praising the host for a very enjoyable event.

* * *

A few days after the banquet, the count read a bizarre news item. From an estate which lay about two hundred miles away from the capital, a large treasure of art and other valuables had disappeared. Fortunately, it was soon found in its original place, except for one golden goblet.

Right-away, the count recalled the banquet at the rabbi's house and the golden goblets. The count did not ponder this for long. He immediately sent his servant to summon Rabbi Löw. The rabbi arrived shortly.

"Listen, Rabbi," the count addressed him without any ado, "it has become very clear to me that you are well-versed in the art of Cabbala. You have knowledge that you have kept secret from me. This time, however, you will not succeed in convincing me otherwise. I have good reason to believe that your abilities in the secret science are great. I'm sure that the reason will not be unknown to you. So, why keep your abilities hidden?"

"Because the Cabbala says, 'You shall not boast of your possessions, for they are passing and useless,'" the rabbi replied. "And although, I do possess some knowledge in this respect, my knowledge is of such an insignificant nature that I am not even allowed to talk about it."

"This time I will hear no excuses," the count retorted. "The reason I called for you is that I want you to initiate me into this science."

The rabbi was taken aback, "I... Your Illustrious Highness... I cannot do that."

"You cannot, or you don't want to?" demanded the count.

"You must understand," the rabbi spoke in a strained voice, "how many grave difficulties relate to practicing this science for Jews, and what difficulties this would bring—you will forgive for saying so—for a non-Jew."

"So that's what the problem is?" the count said, irritated. Well, if that's what it is, then you will just assume your office as my teacher, and that's that. There will be no more excuses. And I'm warning you, Rabbi. Don't provoke my wrath. If you refuse, I swear I will use all my influence and destroy you and your family."

"Very well, as you wish," Rabbi Löw sighed. "Just please have patience, I have a friend in this science, Rabbi don Abraham who lives in Spain. I will require his assistance for such a problematic task."

Then, Rabbi Löw hurried home. At home, he shut himself in his study and pondered what next. Should he write to his friend Rabbi don Abraham? He could hardly imagine Abraham's reaction if he should undertake such a long journey only to be informed that he was to teach the Cabbala to a Christian.

The day was almost at dusk. As if just waking up, the rabbi rose and prepared to attend the synagogue. Because it was Friday, the Saturday service had to begin. Suddenly, a stranger entered the study. He embraced Rabbi Löw and greeted him, "Shalom Aleichem" (peace be with you).

The rabbi could hardly believe his own eyes. The man was none other than Rabbi don Abraham himself. Don Abraham said, "No need to explain anything. I know of your distress, and that's why I am here. I had a dream that revealed to me what you have been through lately. I decided that you needed my help. The trip took only twelve hours; the higher powers led me here. Rest assured, all will turn out well."

Sunday, Rabbi Löw sent the count a message. His friend from Spain was to arrive on Tuesday to begin teaching the count the science of the Cabbala. The rabbi also asked the count to set aside a secret room in his palace for that purpose.

* * *

On the given day, both rabbis went to the count's residence. The Eminent Rabbi then introduced Rabbi don Abraham, his friend and colleague in teaching. Rabbi don Abraham bowed and said, "Please allow me, Your Illustrious Highness, to say a few words before we proceed. The Cabbala has deep roots in a true faith in one being only. It can therefore be practiced only through religion and never without. Only those whose conscience is not burdened with bad deeds can practice it. Those who wish to uncover the veils of secrets and see into the future fearlessly must not have any crime on their consciences. Therefore, consider this: Are you free of all guilt?"

"I am!" the count exclaimed.

"Look behind you," Rabbi don Abraham ordered. "Look!"

The count turned around and looked; he staggered back three steps in fright. Shaking, he muttered remorseful words, "My Lord, have mercy on me!"

"Do you recognize them?" Rabbi Abraham asked.

"My God! They are... my sister and her child..."

The phantom disappeared.

Rabbi Abraham said solemnly, "You are guilty! Your sister and her child died because of you."

The count stood silent. After a few moments, he spoke quietly. "You know my guilt. How you know it, only God, who rules over us all, knows. I must not practice the Cabbala and I know it now; I am not worthy. Only now, I understand your wise words, Rabbi: Divine secrets belong only to the pious. For others it is written, 'Never seek what is unreachable to you; never covet what is hidden.'"

After a short talk, the count thanked both rabbis and bid them farewell. They both returned to Prague with peaceful minds.

17. THE CHILDREN'S CURSE

Once there was a time when many children died in the Jewish Town of Prague. Although, the general belief was that this was God's punishment, it was not clear for what crime the Lord had struck the Jewish community. Therefore, Rabbi Löw summoned one of his Bochers (pupils) and ordered him to go to the Beth Haim (House of Life, i.e. cemetery), where the corpses of children danced on the graves. He was to bring a shroud from one of the dead children. The pupil had no choice but to obey.

At midnight, the graves opened, and out of them, came the children's corpses. They disrobed of their shrouds and began to jump on the graves joyfully. The pupil was a brave young man. He hid behind a large tombstone, and when the opportunity presented itself, he snatched one of the shrouds. He then ran as fast as he could to the rabbi with it.

The rabbi was sitting by an open window. As soon as the pupil had handed him the shroud, the child appeared and begged the rabbi to return the Tachrichim (burial shroud). Without it, the child could not lie in the grave in peace again. The poor child did not speak but only wrung its tiny hands, begging for the shroud.

Rabbi Löw shook his head, "No, I will give you nothing until you tell me why so many children die in our town."

Although the child begged and cried bitterly, the rabbi did not waver from his resolve. Finally, the teary child named four people of the community who lived in sin. Only then, did he receive the shroud back, and he ran back to the cemetery.

The sinners were two couples who led depraved lives. They lived in a street near the rabbi's house. The street was later called Bellesova by the people, because the names of the two lascivious women were Bella and Ella. The guilty people were punished and ceased their lewd conduct. Only then did the plague stop.

18. THE WANDERING ORGAN PLAYER

Behind the impenetrable thickets of black lilac in the Old Town Jewish Cemetery of Prague, on the right bank of the Vltava River, noble dwellers rest in peace. Even those who had turbulent lives are now allowed to dream their eternal dreams in this beautiful garden. The noise of the busy city streets does not reach this Beth Haim (cemetery). Only silence rules there, bowing to the Majesty of Death.

One dead does not rest, however. Born a Jew, he converted to the Catholic faith. He studied Catholic theology and became the Chaplain of St. Vitus Cathedral. Only when his final hour approached did he remember his roots, and he announced that he wished to be put to rest in the Jewish garden of the dead. A young Jewess whom he had once sincerely loved and adored was buried there.

Before his dying, the former chaplain returned to the faith of his fathers, and so after his death, he was buried next to his former lover. Alas, he was not allowed peace. Every night when the clock strikes eleven o'clock, he rises from his grave and rushes to the Vltava riverbank where a skeleton oarsman awaits to take him to the opposite riverbank. There, the derelict chaplain disembarks, and walks uphill to Prague Castle and into the quiet St. Vitus Cathedral, accompanied by the skeleton.

The ex-priest then sits behind the organ and plays, while the skeleton pumps the bellows. Sad tones, moving psalms, and dreamy prophesies permeate the dark nave of the church. The Jewish Catholic priest begs God for forgiveness. In vain.

Before the church clock strikes one in the morning, the organ grows silent again. The organ player and his skeleton companion go back down to the riverbank. Again, they sit in the boat, the skeleton rowing back to the right bank. The doomed organ player then returns to the Old Jewish Cemetery only to repeat his post-mortal duty the next night.

19. Rabbi Rashi

Rabbi Shlomo ben Yitzhak was not even twenty-eight years old when his name had become respected throughout the world. His unique knowledge and scholarship spread his reputation among the nation of Israel to all the countries of the world. He became better known as Rashi, an acronym for Rabban Shel Israel, or Teacher of Israel. He was noted especially for his comprehensive commentary on the Talmud (one of the most important books of the Jewish religion).

His fame reached Prague, and the Talmudic scholar was invited, with the kindest words, to visit Prague, where a renowned Yeshiva (school for the study of Talmud) stood then. Rashi accepted the invitation and arrived in Prague from Palestine. He gave several sermons in a synagogue. His listeners were awed by his erudition.

Rashi was made the First Elder of the great school, and the Jews of Prague were happy to have such a famous man in their midst. Rabbi Rashi then lived happily in the Prague community for an entire year.

However, along with his fame grew the number of his enemies, both Jewish and Gentile. They all envied him his position and respect and worked on his fall.

First, they attempted to make Rabbi Rashi look suspicious before the people by accusing him of hypocrisy and heresy. Then, they tried to denigrate Rashi before the high authorities, claiming that he posed as a Messiah and was thus a public enemy who threatened to lead the Jewish people out of Prague. When all their intrigues had failed, Rashi's enemies decided to eliminate the hated rabbi by murder. A young Talmudist, a Rashi's rival, took the terrible task upon himself.

At that time, Rashi felt anxious because he had been visited by the same dream for three nights. In it, he saw his own funeral. Rabbi Rashi therefore told his wife, "We better leave here, because nothing good awaits us here. A tragedy is about to happen. Should something bad happen to me," he said, "in there," he pointed to an old armoire, "you will find a small vial containing a potion. Don't hesitate whatsoever to use it."

A few days afterwards when Rashi was home alone, the door quietly opened, and in a flash, Rashi's chest was stabbed by a dagger. He cried out, but the dastardly assassin fled. The noise brought the neighbours into the house, and they in turn sent for Rashi's wife.

She rushed into the house and found her husband in a puddle of blood. However, she reacted readily. Opening the armoire, she found the vial and dripped a few drops of the balsamic potion into her husband's wound. The result followed fast—Rashi opened his eyes and spoke to those present, "Stay calm and keep quiet about what you have just witnessed. Tell everyone that I am dead. That way I will be allowed to leave without my enemies persecuting me any further." All present swore to do so.

The people of Prague soon heard that Rabbi Rashi had been assassinated. A great funeral was arranged, and an empty coffin was buried in the Old Town Jewish Cemetery of Prague. Rabbi Rashi left Prague in secret, and he and his wife moved to Regensburg in Bavaria, where they stayed many years. The rabbi built a new Yeshiva school there.

In Rashi's absence, his enemies raised their heads in a renewed hateful campaign against his name. They declared his violent death God's punishment and excommunicated anyone who dared to read his works. To wipe out Rashi's memory completely, they even destroyed his grave and tore down his tombstone. The next day Rashi's grave was found undamaged. In addition, his name was engraved with large gold letters on a tall marble tombstone.

Rashi's enemies believed that Rashi's secret supporters had rebuilt the grave, and they destroyed the grave again. However, the following day, Rashi's grave was found restored again. After this, no one dared to lay a hand on the grave any more. Rashi's enemies became silent, and Rashi was honoured even more than before.

When the news of Rashi's living in Regensburg

reached Prague, people rejoiced, and after Rashi's real death, his body was said to have been brought to Prague and buried in the Old Town Jewish Cemetery.

Many believe that Rashi is buried in a grave with a tombstone that bears the name of Simeon the Just, because another Jewish legend tells the following: Many years after Rashi's death, a rabbi by the name of Simeon the Just died in Prague. He was a man who especially treasured Rashi's work. Simon's disciples went to the cemetery to prepare the grave for their master. When they came to the grave of Rashi, they found it empty. Instead of Shlomo, the tombstone had the name of Simon inscribed on it. The disciples interpreted this as a sign from God to bury their master in Rashi's grave. To this day, many believe that the soul of Rashi was reborn in Tanail Simeon Hazzadik.

20. THE MEISEL SYNAGOGUE

Perhaps the greatest benefactor of the Prague Jews ever was Mordeccai ben Samuel Meisel. He elevated the Jewish community of Prague by his noble service to the spirit of humanity and his love for the people. Meisel (also spelled Maisel) came from a humble background and used his genius to advance justice in his community. To this day, the fruits of his labour can be seen in the Jewish Town of Prague.

Meisel was born in Prague in 1528 as the son of Samuel ben Mair, also called Maisil, and Gitel, the daughter of R. Abraham. Meisel's mother's ascendants were known as pious people whose Prague roots went back for centuries. They were first mentioned in 1474. Though Mordeccai never had children, his parents left several descendants in Prague.

In Meisel's life, two very sad things happened: the expulsion of Jews from Prague by the Emperor Ferdinand I in 1541 and another expulsion in 1561. These events taught young Meisel the hardship of human misery.

After Meisel returned to Prague from exile in March of 1562, better times for Jews arrived. Meisel acquired considerable wealth and respect. The first mention of

Meisel is in a public document, a corporate agreement. In 1580, he formed a business company together with the First Elder of the Jewish community, Yitzhak Rof, also known as Yitzhak the Doctor.

Meisel was a financier of the Imperial Court as well as of the Czech noble estate. He provided loans to the court of Vienna, especially during the Turkish wars. With his loans, the Crown paid soldiers fighting Turkish invaders. Between the years of 1593 and 1598, Meisel was appointed Imperial Counsel, an important government office.

In 1590, Meisel purchased Grunt (land), on which he built a new synagogue. The synagogue was completed at Meisel's expense of ten thousand imperial Thallers in the spring of 1592. This is the famous Meisel Synagogue. Later, Meisel founded a Yeshiva school at the synagogue.

Mordeccai Meisel died between the 13th and 14th of March in 1601. Only twelve days before his death, this unusual man made his last will in the presence of Rabbi Löw ben Bezalel, the Eminent Rabbi, and Elders Joachim Brandeis and Meier Epstein. He designated two co-heirs, his nephews Elias and Simon, who were the sons of Meisel's two brothers. The sons and five daughters of his third brother Salomon were left generous legacies by Meisel.

In 1582, after the death of his first wife Chava, Meisel had married Rof's daughter Frummet. According to an Italian chronicler, when upon his deathbed, Meisel instructed his wife to distribute large sums of money among the poor, she resisted, which led to an ugly scene among the couple.

Meisel's funeral was attended by the highest officials of the Imperial Court; even the emperor was represented. However, the Crown refused to probate Meisel's testament, deciding instead that the last will was invalid because Meisel did not have any direct descendants. In short, all the land, houses, personal property, and money Meisel bequeathed to his relatives became the property of the Crown. During an inventory of the "escheat" property, the government found six hundred thousand imperial Thallers in cash, which was a vast fortune in those times.

The government further ordered all the rabbis in the kingdom to announce in all their temples that they would excommunicate anyone who was a debtor of late Meisel's and failed to report it to the government. A lion's share of the money ended in the pockets of Imperial Chamberlain Philipp Lang, a man infamous for his greed and intrigues. When, in 1609, this top aide of Rudolf II was charged with defrauding imperial coffers, his interrogation revealed this fact.

In 1610, one of Meisel's houses was returned to his family, to Meisel's nephew Jakub Meisel and Jakub's wife Johanka.

After the death of Emperor Rudolf II, Emperor Mathias finally gave the rest of the real estate property left by Meisel's last will back to one of the lawful heirs, to Samuel Meisel Junior. Thus, at least some justice was done after all.

The Jewish community of Prague also fought the estate in a drawn-out legal battle, mostly concerning the land, which the community managed profitably for a long time.

After the death of Samuel Meisel, who bequeathed his property to an orphan by the name of Mark, the latter was finally able to claim all Mordeccai Meisel's inheritance in 1663. Even then, the Meisel Estate litigation was not yet over. In 1665, Mark had to agree not to sell anything that was part of the estate. This is recorded in Prague city books.

The beautiful Meisel Synagogue still stands in Meiselova ulice (Meisel Street) in Prague. In front of it lies a little garden decorated by a wrought iron fence of rare artisanship.

At the end of the 16th century, Meisel built another synagogue, called the High Synagogue. Its entrance is in the court of the Jewish Town Hall, also found in Meisel Street. To enter the actual temple, a visitor must take the stairs leading to the first aboveground floor.

King Wenceslaus I (1230-1253), the brother of St. Agnes of Bohemia, enlarged the Prague under-Castle area by building a new settlement on the right Vltava River bank and had the city encircled by defensive walls. The new part of Prague included the street called Havelska (St. Gallus Street).

In the years of 1232-1234, a new parish church of St. Gallus was built in the area, which was later called St. Gallus New Town. The church was built in the Gothic style, featuring two Old-Bohemian spires in the front, and consisted of three naves. The church building was in a pitiful state when it was handed to the Carmelite Order in 1627. The Carmelites complained about Jewish dealers in second-hand goods, who had built their stalls in the church vicinity and shouted there all day. Allegedly, they often entered the church and caused unpleasant scenes inside. In the summer of 1716, Emperor Charles VI issued a zoning ordinance, ordering that the Jewish stalls be removed from the vicinity of the Church of St. Gallus. Under the pain of severe penalties, Jewish merchants were forbidden to erect new stalls there, and Jews were not allowed even to approach the church.

Later, Jews put their stalls close to the church again;

some of the stalls leaned against the very church walls.

In the summer of 1725, the Old Town City Hall of Prague received an imperial decree, ordering the city authority to keep the Jewish merchants away from the church. In the following years, the ordinance was strictly enforced.

More trouble was started by yet another imperial decree, ordering that the Sacrament of Extreme Unction be carried to the ill and dying in a public procession under canopies and with lights. At first, the Carmelites did not organize such processions. Almost the entire neighbourhood was made up of Jewish residents, and the Carmelite provosts wished to avoid unnecessary friction. However, the 1724 decree ordered that such processions take place in Vienna and Prague.

As soon as a St. Gallus church bell tolled to signal an approaching procession, all Jews were to leave the area, go into the nearest buildings, and stay there until the procession passed. This presented a practical problem for the Jewish merchants, who often had to leave their stalls with their merchandise laid out. Soon, the Carmelite Provost complained that the Jews did not always respect the new rule and that instead of complying, they grumbled about this, loudly enough for everyone to hear.

This time, the Imperial Governor of Bohemia came up with a compromise—Extreme Unction processions would go through the St. Gallus New Town main area on the days when the Jewish merchants did not conduct business there. When they did, the procession would take a different route, through an adjacent monastery and the Golden Wheel Gate in the street of Rytirska. This embittered the Carmelites for a change. The Christians were outraged; they felt insulted by having to take a side route because of the Jews. After much trouble, an understanding was reached between the Old Town Catholics and the Jewish community. The Old Town Council decided that when Jewish merchants conducted their business at the Tandelmarkt (flea market), which was on all days except for Saturdays, Sundays, and holidays, the sacrament would be carried privately and not in a public procession.

With reason, public order and peace returned to St. Gallus neighbourhood. At last, both Christians and Jews realized that none of them benefited from the conflicts.

Emperor Charles IV is said to have erected the cross on the Charles Bridge of Prague. The crucifix was destroyed by a raging mob in Hussite wars on September 10, 1419. In the beginning of the 17th century, the Prague Old Town City Council installed a wooden crucifix in its place.

During the short reign of the "Winter King" Friedrich of Phalz, who was a Calvinist, the crucifix was almost destroyed once again. Friedrich's wife, Elizabeth the English, refused to enter the city if the crucifix stood on the bridge. She urged her husband to remove the cross. However, the people of Prague would not tolerate such desecration. The Old Town City Council therefore posted a strong guard to protect the cross. After the Protestants had been defeated, the Winter King and his English wife fled Prague, riding across the Charles Bridge. The standing crucifix was one of the last things they saw in the capital of Bohemia.

In 1629, Emperor Ferdinand II had a new cross with statues built, and this crucifix was later severely damaged by Swedish bullets during the Swedish siege of Prague. A new statue of the Saviour was cast out of bronze in Hamburg and placed on the wooden cross by an order of Emperor Ferdinand III. The statue was thickly gold-plated.

In the summer of 1696, an Old Town Jew walked by the crucifix, uttering blasphemous remarks. He was arrested and tried. The Royal Court of Appeals sentenced him to pay for a heavily gold-plated metal sign in the Hebrew language around the crucifix. The sign said, "Holy, Holy, and Holy God of the Flocks."

Later, the wooden cross of the crucifix was felled by a violent storm in the summer of 1706. The statue of the Saviour and the Hebrew sign remained standing. Eventually, a metal cross was added to the crucifix, which stands on the Charles Bridge to this day. Two stone statues by sculptor Emanuel Max were erected by the crucifix in 1861. The statues represent Virgin Mary and St. John.

When gas lighting was installed on the Charles Bridge, a set of two lanterns featuring red glass was placed, one on each side of the cross. The cross pedestal was also outfitted with a pretty lamp.

The crucifix pedestal bears three plaques in the Latin, Czech, and German languages, which say, "Thrice Holy, Holy, and Holy to the Honour of Christ the Saviour, as a penalty against a blasphemous Jew, as ordered by the Royal Court of Appeals in the 14th September in the Year of Our Lord 1696."

The Church of Our Lady Before the Tyn, located in Old Town Square has more tombstones in it than any other church in Prague. The people of Prague revere this church deeply. A legend says that in the place of Tyn, the oldest church in Prague once stood, built by the first Czech Christian ruler, Duke Borivoj. St. Ludmila is said to have lived in the church neighbourhood. The earliest written account of the Church of Our Lady Before the Tyn was given in 1135.

The Chapel of the Holy Cross of this church hosts a unique memorial—a red marble slab above the grave of Simon Abeles bears the following inscription: "Simon Abeles, a twelve-year old Jewish boy, following God to the Clementinum College of the Society of Jesus for baptism, sought refuge therein in September 1693. After a few days, he was treacherously lured out of the haven and tempted with promises, threats, beating, and hunger in a dreadful home prison (to make him go back to the Jewish faith). After he had resisted in a strong spirit, he suffered death in the hands of his father and a relative on February 21, 1694. His secretly buried body was unearthed on the sixth day, and until it was laid into a coffin under official supervision, it showed no signs of

109

decay or rigor, while it displayed natural colour and emitted a pleasant smell of rose oil. Then, it was given a solemn funeral by the Old Town Hall, attended by a great number of people, while a special mass was served, and buried here in March 1694."

On May 21, 1810, Emperor Franciscus I, who visited the church, ordered that the body be exhumed and examined. This was performed by a special committee of physicians and spiritual and secular dignitaries. Afterwards, the body was put in the Chapel of St. Ludmila. Following an order of the emperor, the boy's remains were finally reburied in the previous place of rest.

24. THE KLAUS SYNAGOGUE

In the street U stareho hrbitova in Prague 1 District, next to the Jewish Museum and the Old Jewish Cemetery, a simple three-floor building, stands. The Klaus Synagogue is one of the most intriguing monuments of Prague history.

The synagogue fell victim to frequent and devastating fires in the past. Its building breaths sadness, as if it remembered all the Jewish tragedies that had occurred in its vicinity.

Until recently, not much was known about the Klaus Synagogue. Some light was brought into the history of the Klaus Synagogue only shortly before World War II by the work of Dr. Adler, an archivist of the Jewish Town Hall of Prague.

The year of 1561 was a year of oppression and great suffering by Prague Jews, who were expelled from Prague by a decree of Emperor Ferdinand I. On their way out of the city, the Jews were often robbed and killed by highway robbers. The Prague citizens pressed upon the emperor to revoke this decree. However, their pleas were in vain because the emperor once publicly and solemnly swore that he would expel all Jews from Prague for good, and he insisted that he was bound by his oath.

A man by the name of Leo Mordeccai Zemach ben Gerson, a Prague Jew and renowned printer, therefore travelled to Rome to see if the pope himself could help. He was received by the pope and asked him to absolve the emperor from the oath. Pope Pius IV indeed did so, and in 1562, the emperor issued a decree granting the Jews the right to return and live in Prague.

Later, Emperor Maximilian, Ferdinand's son saw to it that the Jewish community of Prague enjoyed his imperial protection.

In the summer of 1571, Maximilian III and his wife Empress Maria visited Prague and the Jewish Town of Prague. The emperor was given a truly royal reception by the community. The noted Rabbi Eliser Ashkenazy welcomed him with a Holy Torah under a baldachin. To commemorate this event, Klaus Synagogue was founded. The name "Klaus" originated in the expression of "closure," meaning a confinement of a divinity student into a room, separated from the world, after the example of Catholic monasteries.

In 1573, the famous Rabbi Löw ben Bezalel was appointed a teacher of Talmud at the Klaus Synagogue. He and his son-in-law Rabbi Chaim Wohl called the synagogue "The Three Klaus Synagogue" because at that time, the synagogue consisted of three small buildings: a yeshiva, which was a seminary or a study house, a Mikvah, which was a bathhouse for ritual purification, and the actual synagogue, a place of worship. Rabbi Löw founded a renowned Talmud seminary there. This synagogue accommodated teachers and students of Talmud and other religious disciplines, who lived in its rooms, not unlike Catholic monks. Klaus Synagogue also bore the name of Beth Hamidrash (House of Prayer).

The famous Rabbi Yitzhak Melling, who had succeeded Rabbi Löw, died in the Klaus Synagogue during a service in the summer of 1583.

In 1689, the synagogue was damaged by a great fire and was rebuilt as one building by Jewish builder Juda Goldschmied de Herz. It was solemnly opened for service on Tuesday of second Tishri 5386 of the Jewish calendar.

Similar Klaus synagogues were also founded later, such as in the German cities of Frankfurt am Main, Halberstadt, Hamburg, Meinz, and Mannheim.

The government of Bohemia dedicated special care to the Klaus Synagogue of Prague. For instance, a decree of the Czech Parliament confirmed Rabbis Elia Spira and Baruch Austerlitz as synagogue ministers in October 19, 1700.

Then, difficult times came. Bohemia was at war with Bavaria and Saxony. In the summer of 1741, the Klaus Synagogue lost its license to conduct religious services and was converted to a grain warehouse. However, after paying the sum of nineteen-hundred imperial Thallers to the government, the synagogue was once again free to offer Jewish religious services.

On May 12, 1820, festive services were performed in the synagogue to celebrate a famous victory of Austria in Italy, and in 1826, another special religious service was conducted in Klaus Synagogue by Rabbi Eleasar Flekles, who prayed for the health and recovery of Emperor Franciscus I.

Another renovation and repair followed in 1863 and 1883 under architect Baum at the cost of 27,350 Austrian ducats. During the years of 1883-1884, the synagogue was further renovated by architect Münzberger, and its original Renaissance style yielded to the Neo-Baroque style. The synagogue ceiling was adorned with stone pomegranates, while a stone acanthus plant was placed upon Corinthian columns.

Throughout its existence, the Klaus Synagogue has been a place of special reverence by the Jews of Prague.

25. The Dancing Jewess

The street leading from Plavecka Street to Trojicka Street under Slovansky vrch in Prague 2 District used to be called Na Ozerove. The river neighbourhood then consisted mainly of wooden huts and vegetable gardens. At the end of the 19th century, blocks of flats were built there, and the area joined the larger Prague downtown.

Where the haunted Ten Maidens House once stood, is a broad road today. Still, a legend tells about a local apparition that so far has refused to leave. The ghost of a dancing Jewess was often seen coming out of the Ten Maidens House and dancing wildly on the street.

One night, a poultry farmer was on his way home from the market. He lived nearby in the Five Kings House in Vysehradska ulice. Having pockets full of cash after a good day at the market, he stopped for a beer or two in a neighbourhood pub. At last, he began to head home. He came to the neighbourhood of Ozerov and said to himself, "What the devil!"

There in front of him, a gorgeous girl danced. Her veil was white as fallen snow, and her rich hair was black as a raven. The girl, her beauty out of this world, danced like the wind, and her skirt flew around her fast-moving hips. The poultry man was taken by her; his blood became strangely warmer and warmer. "Hmm, where do you come from, such a tempting treat?" he mumbled.

In his excitement, he did not pause to think, and instead, ran after her. He grabbed her—she was one hell of a wench, fire and flesh. The poultry farmer was already winking in anticipation of the pleasure. As he was getting ready to whisper a few flirtatious words into her ear, she gripped him with her devilish claws. The poor man could not tell whether he flew over the street or the street moved from under him. Stealing a glance into his dancing companion's face, he exclaimed, "Why, it's the Dancing Jewess!"

The Jewess embraced him with such strength that all the bones in his body cracked. His legs fell out of their joints, and his hair was almost ripped out from its roots by the wild dance. The Jewess danced faster and faster, singing, "Turn the pockets from inside thee, the monster gone will be!"

How, on earth, was he to do that? The Jewess held him in an inescapable grip. Suddenly, it all stopped. The poultry man lay on the street in front of the Ten Maidens House. He could barely move for the pain; he had no hat, no bag, and no walking stick. With a great effort, he managed to drag himself home slowly.

Finally, he made it home. His wife wrung her hands in bewilderment. Even his beard was all curled from the dance from hell. His pockets were completely empty.

The wife started her speech, "You old fool, you stupid lecher, Dancing Jewess my foot! Dancing Jewess in Ozerov! Maybe one that takes money out of the pockets of drunken men like you. I can't believe my husband is an adulterer and a feather-brain!"

The husband sat there, without uttering a syllable and looking as if he just fell out of a mill grinder. Only early in the morning when he recovered his senses, he said to his better half, "Listen, wife, let's go to Ozerov. Maybe we can find some of the money I dropped there last night. It was a true dance from hell, and she kept saying, 'Turn your pockets out... Turn your pockets out...'"

"Right," the wife snapped, "the money left on the street! Are you getting soft in your head?" she said mercilessly. So, the husband went back to sleep.

Because his wife was an early riser, she got up before sunrise. She went to Ozerov. Walking in the street, she tripped over something. She looked, and lo and behold, it was her husband's hat. Then, she found his bag nearby. Something in her mind began to tell her, "What if her husband told the truth?"

On the other end of Ozerov, she found her husband's walking stick. It was still dark, and she looked for the money everywhere, no stone remained unturned. At last, she found a ducat. And another, and another. Eventually, she collected all the money that her husband made at the market the day before. She returned home in a better mood.

The husband slept, and she let him get proper rest. When he woke up in the evening, every bone in his body was aflame. The wife told him about her discovery in Ozerov, "You see I thought what you told me about that dancing Jewess was just a cock-and-bull story. Well, just don't go through Ozerov at night again, understand, darling?"

"No way would I ever forget that," the husband promised to his better half.

The wife then shared the story with a neighbouring housewife.

"For Heaven's Sake!" the neighbour said. "Don't you know how lucky your husband was? My good Lord, the Dancing Jewess could have ripped him to shreds. He was lucky to stumble upon her when she was almost finished with her song before dawn! Once, this unlucky seaman was grabbed by her when she was just beginning. She danced him to death; there were pieces of him all over Ozerov," the neighbour crossed herself.

The poultry man needed a long time to recover from the hellish dance. Others also saw the Dancing Jewess, but they were wise enough to keep away from her.

She was said to fly out of the Ten Maidens House, which was also called "The Kopriva House," after Mr. Kopriva, the proprietor. The dancing ghost always returned to the house when her hour struck. Some even said that there were more such maidens in the same house. They were invisible, but they would not let anyone in the house courtyard; it was as if someone put across an invisible chain.

More legends were told about the ten maidens. In past times, the whole neighbourhood of Podskali was a place of lively commerce with southern European countries; various goods were then shipped on the Vltava River. In those times, a very profitable business of prostitution was established in the neighbourhood. Many rich merchants went to the Ten Maiden House to have a good time. That was not too unusual, except that the brothel was open for business even on the holiest of days. For Christians, the day of Good Friday should be a time for self-reflection even by the worst sinners, and all sin should cease. However, when the entire Christian world commemorated the Saviour and prayed, the Ten Maiden House was nothing but Sodom and Gomorrah.

The merriest of the house girls was one beautiful Jewess. At eleven at night on Good Friday, when she was at her best, singing and dancing, the door opened. In it, appeared a figure clad in a black cloak and holding a whip. "You Godless lot!" he thundered. "Jesus Christ died for you, and you wallow in filth even on Good Friday!"

He began striking all present with the whip. All but

the Jewess fled in fear. She kept mocking the Saviour. The dark figure became enraged and whipped the Jewess out of the house and into the street, "So, dance, you Godless woman! Dance till the Judgment Day!" The figure then disappeared and the beautiful Jewess dances in the street still.

If you, dear reader, happen to be in Prague, you might wish to avoid Ozerov at night. Although the Dancing Jewess has not been sighted there lately, it is better not to risk a dangerous dance.

26. THE WISE RABBI

One day, Rabbi Yechezkel Landau, a famous Prague rabbi, sat in his chair. His face was frowning. In front of him, countless folios lay, some opened, some closed. Suddenly, the rabbi was disturbed in his study. He heard the door's creaking hinges. Two men entered his study. The rabbi recognized Polish compatriots in them, as he was from Poland himself. According to the custom, he greeted them, "Shalom Aleichem."

They exchanged the usual pleasantries, such as "Where are you from?" and "Where are you travelling to?" or "How was your trip?"

"My name is Josef Kohen, the son of Simon Kohen of Warsaw, a wine merchant," the man speaking first began. "This man here is Chaim Geilis, and he has been in my employment for the last five years. Until now, he has always conducted himself well and accompanied me on my business trips. This Rosh Chodesh (the name for the first day of every month in the Hebrew calendar), we were in Austria. I got up from bed and I couldn't find my moneybag. My entire cash, more than one thousand ducats, was in it. Therefore, I called Chaim, who is standing here, and asked him about the moneybag. He, however, gave me an arrogant answer, 'How would you get so much money, since you are only my coachman? Have you robbed someone?'

"What can I do for you?" he asked the two visitors. Because both men answered at the same time, the rabbi asked one of them to speak and the other to be quiet.

"First, I thought that he was just joking, which was unlike him. Then it dawned on me that he was serious. For some reason, he imagined that he was my employer and that I was his coachman. The only thing we agreed upon was to see you so that you could find the real culprit and make a judgment. Most of all, as the one who was cheated, I beg you, Venerable Rabbi, to help me regain my thousand ducats. I have a wife and a child back home, and the thousand ducats is all I have. I was made a beggar."

The first visitor went on in this tone for a long time, until Rabbi Landau told him to stop and let the other man speak.

The other visitor told the same story and claimed that he was the employer and that the other man was his employee.

The rabbi listened and paged in his folios, as if to find an answer in them. Then, he shut the folios and spoke into the conscience of the men standing before him.

Since his speech did not bring any result, the wise rabbi devised a way to trap the faker. He ordered the two men to come back the next day. At the same time, he instructed his servant not to let the visitors into the house the next day.

* * *

At the given hour, both Jews arrived at the rabbi's house. The servant showed them into the hallway and asked them to wait there, because the rabbi could not see them now. They sat down, and while they talked, the rabbi paced in his office. Suddenly, he opened the door and shouted, "Coachman, enter!"

The real Chaim rose and headed for the door. When he realized it was a trap, it was too late. The rabbi received him with a lecture about guilt and punishment. Chaim admitted his guilt and returned the thousand ducats to the rightful owner.

The news of this soon spread throughout the Jewish Town of Prague. Overnight, Rabbi Landau and his two Polish compatriots became local celebrities. Crowds huddled by the rabbi's house to see them. Even the worst enemies of Rabbi Landau were impressed. They dropped their hostilities and became Landau's friends.

* * *

Another legend tells about a verbal fight, Rabbi

Landau had with one of his rivals. The first Sabbath after his arrival in Prague, a Shalosh Sudduth (official luncheon) was given in the rabbi's house, following a custom. Invited were the foremost members of the Jewish community and Old Town dignitaries. Because the rabbi was a man of a tall stature, he often could not reach the table and had to bend down. He made a facetious remark, saying that the table was too low for him. One of the guests took this as an offense to the community and countered, "Not so, Rabbi. Perhaps, the chair is too high for you."

However, since Rabbi Landau had solved the case of the wine merchant and his coachman, few would insult him, and he lived in peace. During his forty years in office, his wisdom and honesty earned him deep respect from the people of Prague. Those who knew Rabbi Landau personally would say, "Zaddik was Nizuz Von Shlomo Hamelech" (The pious man was a spark of Solomon's wisdom).

Rabbi Yechezkel Landau wrote several important works about Jewish law and the Talmud, such as Nodah bi-Yehudah (Known in Judah), Dagul Mervavah (Song of Solomon), and others.

Although there never was a true Russian monastery in Prague, the St. Nicholas Monastery next to the Church of St. Nicholas was called just that. While St. Nicholas Monastery is long gone and forgotten, the Church of St. Nicholas still stands on the corner of Old Town Square.

This magnificent baroque church is one with a rich past. In the 16th century, it was used by Prague Protestants and later by Catholics. In the 19th century, it became a Russian Orthodox church. A huge chandelier, a personal gift of a Russian czar, still hangs in the church as a reminder of that time. Today the church belongs to the Czechoslovak Hussite Church.

St. Nicholas Monastery consisted of three courtyards. The first was square-shaped, light and airy. The other two were narrow, long, and their dark and stale atmosphere gave an impression of a cellar. Three streets led to St. Nicholas Monastery, Parizska, Kaprova, and Meiselova.

The rear tract of the monastery bordered a variety of houses of the Jewish Town of Prague. In the third courtyard the monastery library stood. After the monastery was closed, the library building hosted a theatre until the 1870s. Before the monastery complex was entirely torn down, it served as a glass warehouse. It was a place haunted by the ghost of a Jewess.

Hear this old legend: In the olden times, there was a young monk in the monastery. He was a very handsome lad. Many Christian girls and even one Jewish girl fell in love with him. The Jewish girl often visited him in the monastery. From the house of her parents, a secret passage led into the monastery crypt. There, the lovers met.

The young monk soon fell in love with the Jewish girl, and together, they planned their escape. Their plan was foiled by the monastery abbot. He became suspicious when the young monk spent so much time in the crypt. The abbot followed him and heard the lovers talking about the escape. After the monk had returned from the crypt, the abbot ordered that he be locked in a cell and transferred to another monastery the next morning.

The enchanting Jewess never saw her lover again. She searched for him, thinking that perhaps he fell sick and was in his cell. One night, she entered the monastery through the secret passage and knocked on the cell doors, calling her lover's name. The monks were surprised to hear a woman's voice calling for their missing brother, but since the abbot never told them about the affair, and since they were forbidden to leave their cells at night, they remained clueless.

The Jewess repeated the search the following night, and the following, and the following. The young beauty lost her reason. Desperate with grief, the poor girl sat in the crypt during the day, and at night, she wandered through the monastery. She not only knocked on the cell doors but also tried to open them by force.

One evening, a monk met her in a corridor. She looked ill and emaciated. Only her eyes had fire in them. "Where is Brother Anselm?" she wheezed in the monk's face. He was in shock and could not muster an answer right-away. The Jewess grabbed him by the throat and began strangling him. The monk freed himself and ran to report the incident to the abbot.

The abbot decided to lie in wait for the girl and went into the crypt. He did not have to wait long. Like a real ghost, the Jewish girl appeared out of somewhere and pounced on the abbot, "You killed my Anselm, you monster! You murderer!" she cried, and insanely strong from grief, she choked the abbot with her bony fingers until he was dead.

* * *

In the morning, the monks found the body of their superior. The Jewess was gone. Only now and again, some of the monks saw her at the crypt and in the monastery, where she tried to open the cell doors.

Her ghost has been seen in the area to this day, especially at the former monastery well. Her white-clad, elegant figure sits by the well, embracing her knees with her arms and with her head in her lap.

The abbot did not find peace either; his ghost wanders through the monastery at night. The ghost is known as "The Jesuit."

"**D**id you see him? Late last night, he rushed down to the tower. He must be from far away, who knows from what country."

"No, I saw no one. We slept, but if we were awake we probably wouldn't have seen anything anyway."

"Hmm, you still don't believe me, do you? Well, one time you will. You'll see for yourself that this is the gospel truth."

Thus went a talk of two neighbouring housewives, who sat comfortably on a bench in front of a New Town Market house one summer evening.

"It seems to me, Mrs. Sevler, that you see a great sinner in anyone who does you some damage, a sinner who is condemned never to find peace at that. But you are forgetting that even you might be guilty of some sins for which you will stand before God," Mr. Hradilek, the neighbour cabinetmaker, cut in.

"Men! No respect for anything and always doubting!" Mrs. Sevler snapped back. "I'm telling you I saw him. He ran by the Chapel of Corpus Christi to the city hall, all dishevelled. I knew him right-away, it was Ellbogen the Jew. For what he did to us, he can't have peace even in his grave."

"And what exactly did he do?" inquired the cabinetmaker, who had moved to Prague only recently.

"You don't know?" Mrs. Krep, the other housewife, said. "I'm surprised Sevler here hasn't told you yet. The whole neighbourhood heard the story. God himself knows it's all true. Well, maybe except for Ellbogen's damnation. Who knows, perhaps Ellbogen is alive and well somewhere."

"Or maybe he is dead, and his soul got no peace after it left purgatory and haunts the neighbourhood," finished Mrs. Sevler.

"I think that the only place Ellbogen is haunting is your mind, Mrs. Sevler," remarked the cabinetmaker. "But pray tell what dreadful things the man did to you."

"Oh yes, he hurt us all right. Because of him, my husband died a premature death," Mrs. Sevler took her turn to speak. You know about the measuring cubit that Emperor Charles had installed on the New Town Hall? You will probably remember that this was for anyone who bought fabric and wanted to make certain the merchant didn't cheat them. They would go to the city hall and measure the fabric with the cubit. Yes, it was a wise thing of the emperor to do. But people are just such that they will unjustly turn all that is wise and well-meant to their own benefit."

"How so?" the cabinetmaker asked.

"Well, because the cubit was high on the city hall

130

wall, the New Town councilmen appointed a tall man who stood by and measured the fabric people brought to him for pay. He did well for himself; everyone gave him a nice tip. The man was Ellbogen, which means Elbow in German. Everyone thought that he and his family were honest, but they were not."

"Just because he may have cut a bit of fabric for himself hardly makes him a mortal sinner," interrupted the impatient cabinetmaker.

"But wait, I'm not finished," Mrs. Sevler went on. "About that time, my late husband started a textile business in the Zelinka House in Vodickova ulice. Thank God, we did well. We were the only business of its kind in the whole neighbourhood, so people, including tailors and seamstresses, went to us. However, one day we got an unpleasant surprise. Right across the street, a new textile merchant opened a shop. My husband was depressed about it; he walked about with his head down for a few days. Nevertheless, after a while, it seemed that the new merchant didn't cause any damage to our business. Hardly any customers ever went to the new shop.

"Then, Ellbogen, the cubit attendant, suddenly fell ill. His job was taken over by his son. He was a small young man whom we called 'Little Elbow.' He had to use a ladder to measure the fabric by the cubit. Sometime after that, we noticed that more customers started to go to our competitor. One Sunday afternoon, his shop was packed with people. We were beginning to lose our business. We didn't understand why that was. Old customers of ours didn't come back to us. We did so poorly that we had to go into our modest savings so that we could pay the rent.

"One Sunday morning, my husband happened to walk by the New Town Tower and saw a crowd of people waiting for Ellbogen, Little Elbow, to measure their fabric. He joined the crowd, unnoticed. Soon, a customer handed Ellbogen his fabric to be measured, 'Who did you buy from?' the cubit attendant asked him. He gave the name of our competitor.

"'How many cubits did you buy?'

"'Twenty and a half,' the man answered.

"Ellbogen measured the fabric and said with a smile, 'You got a good deal, and it's an inch more.'

"That wasn't surprising, because we always gave an extra inch too. The surprise came after another customer informed Ellbogen that he had bought from us. Ellbogen measured that fabric and said, frowning, 'It's almost a quarter cubit less than it should be.'

"At that moment, my husband shouted, 'That's a horrible lie and you are a fraud!' and he pushed Ellbogen off his ladder. He then measured the fabric in front of everyone, and it turned out to be a bit more. The crowd began to get restless. My husband became so angry that he cursed the cheating attendant. He came back home, upset and feeling ill, and had to lie down, never to rise again.

"Ellbogen disappeared. I'm sure that he was punished for my husband's death and destroying our livelihood. Now his soul wanders about Prague."

"You mean like the man in the legend of Ahasver the Wandering Jew? Who mocked the Saviour and Lord punished him? So, he had to wander around the world and never found peace?" the cabinetmaker asked.

"Yes, just like that. And if you think that there is no truth in legends, you are very much mistaken," Mrs. Sevler answered.

"Well, be it as it may," Mr. Hradilek, the cabinetmaker said. "It looks like Ellbogen left Prague to avoid punishment."

"You still don't believe me, do you? More people saw him, though. The day before my husband's death, as well as the day of my husband's death, and the day after, Ellbogen always haunts the neighbourhood on those three days. Just wait a moment, we might see him tonight."

"I'm sorry for your sad fate, Mrs. Sevler," the cabinetmaker was shaking his head. "I feel for you for all you have been through. But, I still don't believe in fairy tales. It's possible that God punished that man by death in a foreign land. God's eye sees far and finds a man

133

when he suspects it the least."

Suddenly, it grew dark. "So, if you wish, you wait for Ellbogen. I have to excuse myself; I'm a bit tired," the cabinetmaker concluded and rose to go home inside the building.

When he was in the door, he heard a cry of horror. It was the neighbouring housewives. He ran out in front of the building. To the shock of the neighbours, especially the cabinetmaker, a dark figure with dishevelled hair and beard ran by, toward the New Town Hall. It was Ellbogen, the Ahasver of Prague.

29. FIVE DUCATS FOR SILENCE

During the reign of Empress Maria Theresa, Jews were under suspicion that they supported the King of Prussia and other enemies of the Austrian Empire. In those war times, the Austrian government considered whether to allow Jews to stay in the country or to expel them. The Jews of Prague found out about such intentions and prepared to fight them. Many powerful men and influential friends were approached for help.

One day the butler of Count Leopold Krakovsky of Kolowrat answered the door and saw a man whom he did not know. The stranger asked whether he could speak to the count. Count Kolowrat guessed what it was about, so he instructed the butler to brush off the visitor. The man left with a sad expression.

He was, however, back after some time and told the butler he would give him five ducats if the butler arranged a meeting with the count. Moreover, the stranger told the butler that he would say his request in no more than one mere word to the count. When the count heard this, he was intrigued. He agreed; besides, let the butler have his tip. No more than one word, though! The visitor was ushered in.

Without speaking, he bowed, with respect that was

due to an imperial government minister in those times. He then said, "Schweigen," which means "keep silent" in German. He bowed again and left. The visitor was a Prague Jew.

Sometime after that, a government conference took place. It was presided by Empress Maria Theresa. Among the issues dealt with was an expulsion of Jews from Prague. Some spoke in favour of the measure, some against it. Count Kounic fiercely defended the Jews, while Count Kolowrat kept quiet. The empress noticed that, and after Count Kounic had finished his speech, she said, "My dear Kolowrat, why are you so reticent? Why don't you share your thoughts with us?"

"You see, Your Majesty," Count Kolowrat replied, "I have been thinking about this: My butler got five ducats if I don't speak. I wonder how much Kounic's butler got for his master's speaking."

The evening was already casting its shadows on the Jewish ghetto of Prague one summer day of 1768. It was the time between Minchah (afternoon prayer) and Maariv (evening prayer). Rädlech were forming in the streets—groups of ghetto residents who chatted to spend their free time until the end of Sabbath.

The lack of newspapers was in those times filled by sharing the news by word of mouth. One ghetto resident was an especially competent "reporter." His oral presentations of leading news earned him the nickname of "Laudon," after a famous Austrian cavalry general. Another "reporter" by the name of David Sepkes was a street columnist. Crowds gathered to listen to his interpretations of the week's events. The daily news was more than sufficiently supplied by female ghetto residents. A passer-by could learn practically anything on the streets then; there was no need to read a paper.

"Today was Oneg Shabes (a great Saturday)," announced the street reporter. His bony figure turned around to see all his listeners. "As long as our temple has stood, we haven't heard more beautiful singing by a Chazzan (cantor)."

"Certainly," one older resident remarked, "the new

cantor sings beautifully, but I still think that injustice was done to our old Naftali. He is such a decent and just man, and the temple leaves him unemployed and hires a foreigner instead."

"Kowed, divine grace, is above everything," replied Laudon. "And what do you think, Rav Sorech, since we brought our rabbi all the way from Poland and entrusted him with our community, why not bring the cantor from there as well? If he can sing such Kedushe (sacrament), he must have Kedushe in his body." Laudon paused, clicking his tongue in satisfaction and receiving nods and voices of agreement from the crowd. Laudon got on his high horse and added, "Besides, why does Naftali need to be a cantor? He has no children anyway."

A painful sigh crossed Rav Sorech's lips. Everyone present knew that only six months ago, poor Sorech buried his only son who had fallen to fever. A live wound was opened afresh by the reporter's remark, and Rav Sorech exclaimed, "A man who has no children wants to live too, and his wife needs to eat! Naftali is a scholar, who travelled through the whole of Ashkenazy (Germany), and he is an honest man and a proper Shliach Zibbur (designated cantor). He never clouded the waters of this community. None of you here know what I know. Cantor Naftali's sister would have died from hunger a long time ago, had Naftali not given her all the food from his own kitchen. You cannot let such a man down. And let me tell something else as well."

The eyes of the old Rav Sorech watched everyone in the crowd. "With all due respect, the new cantor has the voice of Jacob, but his hands are the hands of Esau!"

The debate would have gone on, if it had not been for one listener who pointed to the synagogue servant passing by and said that it was time for Maariv, an evening prayer.

* * *

The night darkness had already set upon the streets when Mayor Israel Frankl was leaving the temple. The Frankls were a family of Jewish patricians, in whom, for generations, intelligence united with nobility of spirit and natural kindness. They were direct descendants of the famous Jewish family of Spira (Spiro, Shapiro) who supported education in Jewish communities in the Middle Ages and who helped the Czech economy by building the first silk industry in Bohemia.

Because of the family merit in elevating the Jewish community, the Jewish Town of Prague elected Simon Volf Frankl, Israel's father, the mayor. After his father's tragic death, Israel Frankl became the mayor after his father. Simon Volf Frankl, the father, died by his own hand, hanging himself. He was a famous, but much maligned man. His enemies spread ugly accusations that he was an agent of Prussian King Friedrich the Great and thus a traitor. The talk even reached Empress Maria Theresa.

When Israel Frankl, the new mayor, arrived home, his wife Frummet was expecting him. She put wine and candles on the table so that he could perform Habdalah (a ceremony concluding the Sabbath holiday). Frankl entered with his usual greeting and squeezed his wife's hand.

The husband and wife were both tall, handsome people. The mayor looked at his wife lovingly. A lit Habdalah candle cast light on the mayor's face. It was a remarkable face. His raven black hair was rich, greying on his temples, although the mayor was only forty-five years old. His intelligent forehead was full of wrinkles, betraying pain and sadness. His long and narrow nose and his iron-shaped chin spoke of great will and energy.

Frummet, who was ten years younger than her husband, was a contrast to her husband's solemnity. Her kind round face and her brown eyes radiated vitality.

Raising a cup of wine, Israel Frankl prayed over a candle flame for blessing of the ending Sabbath. When he touched the wine, he called, "To a good and happy week!"

Frummet who had joined her husband in the festivity then rushed to an armoire. She opened it, took out a letter with a large seal, and gave it to her husband,

"My dear Israel, this is a letter for you from the government." The mayor opened the letter, sat by a lamp and read it in a hurry. His face grew pale.

"Shemah Yisroel," (listen Israel) his wife said. "What is it?" Worriedly, she rubbed a few drops of wine into his grey temples and lovingly caressed his temples and forehead.

After a moment or two, her husband recovered and said quietly, "Don't be alarmed, dear Frummet. I was just a bit overwhelmed by this news. I am fine now. It's just that we might get a special visitor," he continued. "The son of Empress Maria Theresa, Emperor Joseph, is travelling through Bohemia. Chances are he might want to visit the Jewish Town of Prague. I am to make sure that he receives a nice welcome and that he only finds order and clean streets here.

"Well, you know that my father Zichrono Livrocho (of blessed memory) had welcomed Joseph here in the past. That was at the event of Joseph's twenty-seventh birthday. You probably also remember what kind of trouble this brought to our Kehille (community). Yes, the sovereign was given a great birthday party here and was very impressed. However, some people then resented this out of jealousy and did their best to throw as much filth on Prague Jews as they could. They slandered my poor father with the Empress, accusing him of all kind of nonsense and finally drove him to suicide. And now," the

141

mayor's face frowned again, "the sovereign wants to come here as a private person and an independent observer. I cannot even imagine the problems this could mean."

"That's exactly why, my dear husband," said Frummet, "you must fortify yourself with great patience. Let us not worry prematurely—Emperor Joseph is known as a fair man who cares about people. Besides, don't you remember when you tried to resign from your office four years ago, the Empress herself refused to accept it, writing to the Government of Bohemia that she couldn't do without your exemplary service? If something goes wrong, you can always defend yourself with her letter. Although," Frummet sighed, "dear Almighty knows how easy we and our children could live without the burden of your office."

The mayor stood up and put his hand on Frummet's shoulder, "My beloved wife," he said, "I am not even worried about myself but rather about the community. I'm going to see our learned Rav (rabbi). He might have some ideas about how to handle this. Also, I will get an appointment with the Imperial Governor. No one must learn of the emperor's incognito visit lest the community becomes excited or nervous. That wouldn't go well with the Emperor because he wants to surprise us and to avoid being recognized, at least for some time."

Mayor Frankl then put the letter into his pocket.

After wrapping himself in a warm coat and kissing his wife, he left home.

* * *

At the same time, Naftali, the former cantor, arrived at his humble abode in Pinkas Street. The Jewish community had provided the home to him free of charge. Naftali and his wife Gella had lived there ever since he became a Chazzan (cantor). Although the flat was small and somewhat dark and damp, Naftali was not a man of demanding nature and was happy there. In addition, the flat hid a treasure—a rare collection of books Naftali inherited after his grandfather Naftali Katz, a Lublin rabbi. As often as he could, Naftali tried to enlarge his library. This was not easy, especially lately, since he had to help the family of his widowed sister.

Naftali was more than sixty years old, but his straight figure, his dark hair, and his youthful face of a Sephardic Jew did not betray his age. As a fifteen-year old boy, Naftali had travelled throughout the world. He had to use his Matona, his gift of a singing voice, to support himself and his impoverished mother. The knowledge of people he had gathered during his life of travel and through a study of Jewish scripts led him to adopt a life philosophy of quiet resignation. He was at ease with the world and its people.

Only one thing troubled Naftali's soul—his marriage remained childless. Otherwise, his marriage with Gella was a happy one. His wife, whom he learned to know and love in Bavaria, was a beautiful woman. Her education was also unique for a Jewish woman in those times—she knew all the fundamental Jewish books in both Hebrew and German. Reading of these scripts was her only spiritual refreshment after looking after a household and her husband.

When Naftali was at home in the Semiroth (singing), he often sang an apotheosis in praise of the Jewish woman. The house then sounded with "He Who Found a Good Woman," while Naftali was looking with love at his wife and partner in life. If Naftali occasionally decried the unfair Fate, "What am I doing in the world when I am nothing but an infertile tree?"

His wife Frummet soothed him, "Don't you know, dear husband, that it is written, 'The infertile should not say, see, I am like dry grass? For I shall give you your name, says the Eternal.' Are you not, Naftali, my dearest, indeed the Shliah Zibbur (designated cantor) who delivers the wishes and prayers of his community to the Throne of the Lord? Are you not a Chazzan (cantor) who is renowned throughout the world?"

Naftali did not sing for a few days and was immersed in meditation. The reason was that sympathetic neighbours and friends had secretly informed the couple that the temple elders had decided to fire Naftali and hire a new cantor. Gella noticed that her husband was still kind and helpful to the new cantor who was arrogant, and that Naftali took it with dignity. She knew, however, that deep inside, he suffered greatly from the injustice.

For the entire Saturday, Naftali and his wife Gella kept calm. They did not wish to disturb the peace of the holy day. Now the day was over and the calm with it. Gella spoke to her husband, "Naftali, my dearest, is it really true what people say? That some who-knows-from-where Pole takes your job and you take it sitting down? After you have been in the office in Meisel Synagogue and the School for twenty years?"

In answering her, Naftali took out Sheloh ("That Is Yours," a prayer) from a large folio that lay before him and said, "It's enough what I hear from people, and you my wife wish perhaps to torment me in a matter which I must accept as a test from the Lord and which I cannot change? Do you want me to go before the Gabboyim (the elders) and accuse them? Who would be the judge? I have no choice but to suffer it, even though I know that injustice has been done to me, and on top of that I have no idea how I will be able to help the poor Yesomim (orphans) of my late brother-in-law now."

Upset, he rose, and after walking around the room for a minute or two, he sighed, "The new cantor can produce sounds beautiful for the ear, but he has heart for nothing. I could tell that right-away. Dibbur (speech of the heart) is the most important thing for a cantor, and he doesn't have it in him. Still, every Shames (servant) and Balbos (master) who have a daughter to marry now speculate about the new cantor. People just will be fooled by flattery and smooth sounds. There is no way to fight it."

To which Gella replied, "The Book of Gemmara says, 'Even if your wife is small, lean on her.' Why don't you share your grief with me? Why do I have to wait for what people tell me? Why don't you go see the rabbi and let him help you? Hopefully, he will defend your case."

"If you must know, Gella, the rabbi talked to me about that already. Yesterday, he sent his servant to me to borrow a Sefer (a book) from me. You know how klutzy the servant is, he keeps dropping things. I didn't want to risk his dropping my rare book, so I took it to the rabbi myself. The rabbi welcomed me heartily and asked, too, whether it was true that the temple elders wanted to fire me after my twenty-year service and hire a new cantor. I told him, 'Yes, I know about it, but as you know Rebbe, the temple elders are free to fire and hire anyone they please, twenty-year-service or not.'"

"Not necessarily," said the rabbi. "Because, if they fire you, they are committing a great Avle (injustice) against you. I will do everything within my powers to change the elders' minds about this so that you are rewarded for your work in your old age."

"Is that what he said?" exclaimed Gella. "Long live the Rav! He will keep his word."

Naftali, it seemed, did not share his wife's confidence. He shrugged his shoulders and said resignedly, "Well, the elders will not be softened, not even by a hundred Rabbonim (rabbis)." He then began reading in his Sheloh. Gella did not say anything.

* * *

Rabbi Ezekiel Landau sat in his large library, which also served as his study and office. The rabbi was surrounded by a great arsenal of Jewish learning; books and folia lay piled everywhere, even on his desk next to an old-fashioned inkwell.

After the Sabbath was over, Rabbi Landau rushed back to his writing, which he would later publish. His book was a contribution to the Halakhic literature (on Jewish religious law).

The rabbi's thoughts were interrupted. A surprise visit by Mayor Israel Frankl was announced. The unexpected visitor soon entered the rabbi's study.

"Boruch Habboch Mekhas," (Be greeted you who enter) Rabbi Landau greeted the mayor and offered him a chair.

"Rebbe, you must be wondering," the mayor began,

147

"why I come here at such an hour, and I ask you to forgive me for that. However, there is a matter of the utmost importance for the community, a matter in which I hope to receive your advice."

The rabbi bowed slightly from his chair, and the mayor proceeded to explain, speaking with a tone that betrayed his nervousness. "First I must go back in time. Rebbe certainly remembers that our community suffered greatly twenty-four years ago. My father, Sichrono Livrocho, was the mayor then. Rebbe will also remember that my late father then organized a splendid ceremony for Prague to welcome Prince Joseph, who is our emperor today. Today I know that many tried to dissuade my father from such enterprise, among them Reb Salme Koref. They argued that displaying so much splendour would be boasting of our wealth and this would provoke jealousy, if not hatred, toward the community. Unfortunately, what followed proved them right.

"We both know what tragedy our Kehille had to go through then, and what effort it cost us even to be able to return home to Prague. When all of us had faced expulsion from Prague, my father tried his best to change that unfortunate imperial decree. He even turned to foreign countries for help, only to end up being accused of being a German spy. He died an unhappy broken man.

"Rebbe, do you remember those horrible times—

148

how many people lost their homes and their livelihoods? How many people died in poverty in the country, exiled from Prague and how many families wound up in poverty?"

The rabbi was listening carefully. He nodded.

"Yes, Rebbe," the paled mayor said, "I have come here today to open an old wound. I want to open your tortured heart and let it bleed afresh again. I have no choice. It was on Friday when I, a young Balbos (gentleman), and a newly married man, went to my father to the synagogue for his Benshen (blessing). He blessed me in a great ceremony, and afterward he told me to sit down and listen. He then said, 'Dear son, I have never asked you for anything, but today I must do so, and I hope you will not remain deaf to my wish.'

"To which I replied, 'Certainly, father. If it's possible I will do what you ask me.' He said, 'Very well, then. You know, my son, that I am very tired of the burden of my office. I will resign, and I want you to take it over.'"

"I stood there dumbfounded. I wished to help my father and I said, 'But father, there are much more experienced and competent men for such office in the community, such as Reb Salme Koref and...'

"'Reb Salme Koref,' my father cut in, just told me there was no way he would ever take the office. Moreover, I begged him practically on my knees. No, he won't do it. I then looked and looked for the right man

149

here and there, as Moshe Rabbenau says, and saw only you my dearest son, my pride. You can take the burden off my shoulders; I am no longer a giant.'"

"Believe me Rav," Mayor Frankl interrupted his own storytelling, "I still see my father in my nightmares. He sits there before me and tears are running down his face."

The mayor sighed and looked the rabbi in the face. The rabbi gave a start. He saw that the mayor was crying. "Mekhas," (Your Excellency) Rabbi Landau said, "you are committing a sin if you live in your own grief, for indeed you won't find anything good in such sad memories."

"Then, Rebbe, let me unburden my heart to you," the mayor said. "Except for my wife, you are the first one to hear this. And because I am asking for your advice, I will tell you everything." The mayor continued the story, this time in a calmer voice, "After my father had asked me this, I thought, 'How can you, a son of such a noble father be the first and let him be behind? How would this look before God and the community?' And I told my father that I didn't feel mature nor competent for such an office of great responsibility."

"My father replied bitterly, 'I see. You think just as our old ones used to say—a new dominion must be separated from the old one. If I bid farewell to this valley of tears, you must become my successor.'

150

"I threw myself at my father's feet, begging him to chase away his sadness and to remain the administrator of the community. I left with a wrong impression, thinking that everything would be all right, and that my father had listened to my reasoning after all. The Sabbath morning, however, gave me a terrible surprise—news that deprived me of joy of life forever."

The rabbi was listening with the utmost attention, and the mayor went on, "Before I entered the synagogue that day, I was told that my father was very ill and was bedridden. This was to prepare me for much worse news yet. When I entered my father's home, I found gathered members of Chevra Kadisha (burial society) there. Reb Salme Koref took me to my father's study and uncovered the horrible truth. My father had taken his own life on Holy Shabes. My father was Menus Azmo Lodaas (he who killed himself knowingly).

"As if in a bad dream, I staggered back into the ceremonial room, followed by Koref. My father's body was ready for burial. On the table near him, was an open book, Baba Mezia Gemmara, (A tract of Talmud, Part II, Jewish Civil Law), and on one page lay my father's gold watch. Reb Salme lifted the watch from the book and pointed to the page. It read, 'It is a duty to fulfil a wish of the deceased.'"

"I collapsed and lost consciousness. Someone carried me home. I fell ill, seriously enough that some thought I wouldn't live. With God's help, I recovered, though. After Shloshim (thirty days after a person's death), a delegation from the community came to my house, headed by Reb Salme Koref. They begged me to accept my father's vacant office.

"I wanted to refuse vehemently, but Reb Koref raised his forefinger and said, 'It is your duty to obey a wish of the deceased.' So, I accepted. Ever since, I have been the mayor, and God is my witness that I have tried my best to restore the community to the prosperity it once knew. I don't want to, and I must not praise myself. However, you know that my work was recognized even by Her Imperial Majesty, but ever since, I have lived with a bitter idea that my words to my father may have sent him to his death.

"If only then I could have obeyed him as a good son, he probably wouldn't have taken such a desperate step." Mayor Frankl wiped beads of sweat off his forehead and looked at the rabbi questioningly.

Rabbi Landau rose from his chair and looked the mayor in the eye. He nodded, and after a moment or two he said, "Mekhas Reb Yisroel, do you believe in divine will which a mere mortal cannot fight?"

"I certainly do, Rebbe," answered the mayor, "with all my being. What decent Jew wouldn't?"

"Then, know," the rabbi said in a gentle but persuasive voice, "that your father, Sichrono Livrocho,

152

only met his Fate. You blame yourself unjustly. Even if your father saw you becoming the mayor, he would have ended the same way in his mental illness. This way he didn't have to suffer even more humiliation." The rabbi went on, "If your resistance to your father's request was only healthy and justified; your blaming yourself is not!"

Mayor Frankl was shaking, and tears ran down his face. When he gathered himself enough to speak, he said at last, "Thank you, Rebbe, a thousand times! I feel much better now. Why haven't I listened to such words before? How many bitter hours could I have been spared?"

"Was this the Ezoh (advice) you sought from me?" the rabbi inquired.

"No, Rebbe, there is more," the mayor sighed and took the official letter from his pocket. He showed it to the rabbi and explained his worries. "The fact that the emperor is travelling incognito worries me the most. If anything goes wrong, it could have tragic consequences for the community. We still remember what troubles were brought upon us by the emperor's birthday celebration all those years ago," the mayor concluded his speech.

The rabbi's face bore a slight smile. He said, "Mekhas, you know that Shlomeh Melech (Jewish King Solomon) says, 'the heart of a king is like the springs in God's hands.' But why does the wise Solomon compare a stream of water with a human heart?" the rabbi went on.

"Because water, just like the heart of a king, is a natural element that can bring well-being for people but can also become a force of disaster, destroying everything in its way.

"It was divine will that the heart of the empress wreaked havoc upon this community during your father's administration. You remember learning for what sins the Jews were punished by the destruction of their holy places in the past. Today, however, the Prague Jews are not guilty of sins against morality, law, or customs. As a spiritual leader of this community, I can assure you that Prague has now become an Ir Veem Beyisroel (Mother City of Israel) more than ever before. Just as the heart of the empress was set against us then, the heart of the emperor can be a blessing for us now.

"You as the mayor, you stand before God with a clean conscience; you have worked hard for this town; you have helped the poor, the widows and orphans. Then what do your worries and anxieties mean? That perhaps there is still injustice among us. There indeed may be one that can become an accusation of our community before the Almighty. You are a man who can still remedy it. Do that and an accuser won't have ground to stand on," the rabbi finished.

The mayor's eyes shone, and he said in a determined voice, "I give you my word, Rebbe, that I will try to correct anything you judge unjust in this community!"

"Then listen," said the rabbi, "Cantor Naftali is a modest and good man who worked in the Old and Meisel Synagogues for the last twenty-five years. Also, he has had to support his impoverished sister's family with his meagre income. Despite all this, the Gabboim now want to fire him and hire a new cantor. Naftali is a Lambden, a man dedicated to God, but it must hurt him deeply to lose his job in his old age, and to leave the places he had been singing and praying. You must admit that this is an injustice crying to the heavens. Yes, I am asking you to prevent it," finished the rabbi.

The mayor rested his chin on his hand and was silent for a moment. Then he spoke, "Yes, Rebbe, I understand. The thing is, though, that my influence has its limits. I am almost wondering whether my engagement in the matter might not irritate the elders to the point that they would become even more reckless. Yes, my late father, too, always complained about the elders having too much power. He used to say that their arbitrary decisions hurt the community.

"There are so many schools of thought and so many elders and various committees in this community of ours that I doubt I can do much. But I will do what I can, I promise you that." The mayor stopped his speech, and he turned to the rabbi again, touched, "Thank you so much for your words of encouragement and consolation. I feel as if an angel of mercy touched my soul. There is wisdom in your words. That is why I would like to ask you for your counsel in one more matter."

Here, the mayor told the rabbi about his appointment with the Imperial Governor the next day. It was a dark night when the two most respected members of the Jewish Town of Prague bid their farewells to each other.

* * *

The streets of Prague and their residents seemed different the next day. Nervous excitement was everywhere. Since people back then lived not only together but also for each other, no event went unnoticed. Public sensation was created when the mayor's carriage was seen driving out of the ghetto's gate. David Sepkes, the ghetto street "reporter" speculated that something important was afoot, especially since he also knew that the mayor went to see the rabbi last night and stayed there for a long time.

At noon, the mayor's carriage returned to the ghetto and stopped by Rabbi Landau's house. The mayor stepped out of the carriage and rushed up the stairs to the rabbi's door. This calmed the anxiety—whatever was going on, just the fact that Rabbi Landau participated in it was reassuring.

A beaming Mayor Frankl was shown to the study by

the rabbi, who asked, "Well, Rebbe, how did the appointment with the governor go?"

The mayor replied, smiling, "I think I have nothing but good news to report. That was exactly what Imperial Governor Count Schaffgotsch told me. He said that he had written to the emperor about the matter and that His Imperial Majesty changed his mind about his visit. After careful consideration, the emperor decided to stay in Vienna—he had important state matters to attend to anyway. You can well imagine, Rebbe," the mayor went on, "what a relief this was for me. I could barely stutter to the governor that the Prague Jewish Community will lose a great honour of His Majesty's visit, and to assure Vienna of our great devotion to the Imperial Court.

"The count was in a good and friendly mood, one I haven't seen him in for a long time. He patted me on the shoulder and said, 'Dear Mayor Frankl, the Jewish community can be happy to have a mayor like yourself. After all the disasters of the recent past, it seems to be doing really well.'

"And just when I was ready to leave," the mayor continued his narration, "the governor asked me if there was anything else he could do for me. I replied, 'Yes, there actually is, Your Excellency,' and I told him about Cantor Naftali and asked him whether he could help to save the great man from humiliation and poverty, perhaps by issuing a gubernatorial decree, one that both the Meisel Synagogue and the Old-New Synagogue elders would be bound by.

"The governor nodded and said, 'You are a kind man, Frankl. You always care about the others but never ask anything for yourself. I wish there were more people like you.' After I had given the governor all the relevant information, he himself wrote a decree, ordering the synagogue elders to continue Naftali's pay."

"Dear Reb Yisroel," the rabbi said, "May the Almighty spare you trouble and sorrow just as you saved this community from injustice."

The rabbi embraced the mayor and walked him to the door—the mayor could hardly wait to share the good news with his wife Frummet.

* * *

Another week passed, and Sabbath arrived. Once again, before the Maariv prayer, people gathered in the usual place to hear the news from "Laudon," the street news teller. They learned about the surprise old Cantor Naftali got. A governor's messenger brought him a letter, informing him that Naftali was, upon Mayor Frankl's recommendation, appointed a Kohl Chazzan, and that the communities of the Meisel and the Old-New Synagogue were to pay him three Viennese ducats a week for the rest of his life.

"You see now," spoke Reb Sorech, "our mayor was able to take care that injustice wasn't done to the old cantor after all." Reb Sorech smiled, "I am sure you also heard of the new cantor's hasty departure."

"O yes, that's another good one!" said David Sepkes, also a street reporter, with a roguish twinkle in his eye. "I am sure you, Laudon, will be especially interested to hear it. It was your sister Almone Sprinzel, was it not, who had sent many Shadhonim (marriage brokers) to that young Pole?"

"Tell us, David," the people demanded, while "Laudon" snuck away to join another group.

"This week an old Polish Jew visited the Gabbe (a synagogue elder) of the Old-New Synagogue and asked for Leeman Rachamim (help). He wanted the elder to help him find his son-in-law who was a travelling cantor and who had left his wife and children a year ago. And yes, the man in question was, indeed, our new cantor."

David Sepkes paused, but the news-hungry crowd urged him to continue.

"Well, they found the young Pole in his hostel. He had hardly any time to say farewells because his father-in-law took him with him right-away. Now, you can well imagine the long faces of all the Rabbosai (gentlemen) who wanted the new cantor as a suitor for their daughters. In the end they were glad the old cantor hadn't handed them his resignation."

The time for the Maariv prayer was near, and the listeners left.

* * *

Naftali's relatives treasured the gubernatorial letter of appointment for generations. The prediction of Rabbi Landau that the heart of the emperor would be kind to the people of Israel became fulfilled.

Twelve years later in 1780, Emperor Joseph II visited the Prague Jewish Town. This time, his visit brought new blessings for the Jews of Prague—the emperor was responsible for the legal reforms, which gave the Czech Jews civil rights they never enjoyed before.

Israel Frankl did not live to see the blessed reforms. A few years before, the good mayor had closed his eyes forever and joined his beloved wife Frummet in the Old Jewish Cemetery. There, they dream their eternal dream together.

Also by Sharpless House

THE MEMOIRS OF A PRAGUE EXECUTIONER

A Historical Novel Based on Actual Events

A young man is about to graduate from medical school when a sudden shift of fate changes his life forever. He becomes stuck in the most detested profession for the rest of his life, and he is on his way to becoming the most well-known executioner in the history of Bohemia.

Master Jan finds himself in the centre of the historical events of the time. The religious and political turmoil of Bohemia culminates in the 1621 White Mountain Battle. Czech Protestant rebels are defeated by Catholic forces, and Master Jan is to execute 27 men who are his fellow Protestants.

The Old Town Executioner gives the reader a first hand account about how justice was carried out by the medieval law. While his memoirs offer an intriguing account of the manners and values of late medieval society, his observations about human nature may come as a surprise. The law and society have changed since the 17th century, but people have changed very little.

PRAGUE MYSTERIES

Crime Stories by Czech Authors

Prague is now one of the most popular tourist destinations of the world. Every year, the capital of the Czech Republic attracts visitors by the millions. Many claim that Prague is one of the most beautiful and intriguing cities they have ever seen.

Czech history goes back more than a thousand years, and the Czech people have gone through very turbulent times. The country has had its ups and downs. In the 14th century, Prague was the seat of Emperor Charles IV and the political powerhouse of Central Europe. In the 16th century, Prague was the cultural capital of Europe under the rule of Emperor Rudolf II. The twentieth century saw Czechs fall first under Nazi occupation and then under the Soviet rule. It was not until 1989 when the Czechs were able to live in freedom again.

Yet, Prague and the Czech Republic still remain somewhat of an enigma to many. This collection of short crime stories offers the reader a chance to learn more about the Czech psyche, while having fun reading mysteries by such authors as Karel Capek, Jaroslav Hasek or Franz Kafka. Many of the stories have never been translated into English until now.